GW00871151

BERNARD ASHLEY was born in Woolwich, South London, and grew up there and in the Medway Towns. He is a Head Teacher with the Inner London Education Authority, living in Charlton.

He has written ten novels, as well as books for younger children. Two novels have previously been televised, *Break in the Sun* and *Running Scared*. *The Country Boy* is currently being televised in six parts by BBC Television and the cover shows Jeremy Sweetland as he appears in the part of Ben.

Also by Bernard Ashley

The Trouble with Donovan Croft
Terry on the Fence
All My Men
A Kind of Wild Justice
Break in the Sun
(All published by Oxford University Press)

Dodgem
High Pavement Blues
Janey
Running Scared
Bad Blood
Dinner Ladies Don't Count (Blackbird)
Linda's Lie (Blackbird)
Your Guess is as Good as Mine (Redwing)
(Published by Julia MacRae Books)

THE COUNTRY BOY

by

Bernard Ashley

MILLTOWN N.S
RATHCONRATH
MULLINGAR

Copyright © Bernard Ashley 1989
All rights reserved
First published in Great Britain 1989
by Julia MacRae Books
A division of Walker Books Limited
87 Vauxhall Walk, London, SE11 5HJ

British Library Cataloguing in Publication Data
Ashley, Bernard
The country boy
823'.914 [F]

ISBN 0-86203-387-X

Printed and bound in Great Britain by/
Richard Clay (St. Ives Group plc), Bungay, Suffolk.

CAST LIST

BEN	Jeremy Sweetland
SALLY	Siobhan Burke
DAVE	Nigel Humphreys
LYN	Helen Duvall
ALICE	Mary Wimbush
DR. SKELLMAN	Bronwyn Baud
CHARMAINE	Claire Callaghan
WEST	Marc Sinden
BARBARA	Janet Palmer
ADAM	Mark Burdis
SCOT	Joe Mullaney
BRIT	Tony London
MARTOUF	Barry Houghton
JOHNSON-MARSHALL	John Barcroft
MRS. JOHNSON-MARSHALL	Lollie May
BILL	Peter Barnes
TED	Eric Mason
DR. REID	Lisa Simone
TONY	Robert Kenley
SISTER O'HARA	Geraldine Griffiths
PILK	Paul Jayson
DIV	Gary Powell
BAZ	Sean Murray
IRAJ	David Adams
W.P.C.	Frankie Jordan
MRS. CRADDOCK	Leila Hoffman
MURRAY-MOTT	Chris Whittingham
ANALYST	Robert Craig Morgan
SKIPPER	Will Kenton
LEE	Alan Dean
KELLY	Alice Dawnay
LISA	Patsy Palmer
JO	Nikky Gordon
DUKE	Roger
JEM	Mierny

FOREWORD

A screenplay is a product of partnerships. While a novel is
nursed in secrecy, perhaps its theme or its outline being
shared with a publisher, the film or television play has
several partners in the writing process who have an active
say in what will happen. A novel can go to China or to
outer space, but a TV serial might have to happen within
easy reach of the Television Centre: a book might have a
cast of thousands, a TV play no more than ten or fifteen.
Whatever fanciful ideas a writer might have, somebody
has to make them look as if they're happening, and
somebody else has to pay for it. The television writing
team, then, consists of the writer, the producer and the
director. It is the producer's job to keep over-all control
of the project, which includes overseeing the money and
the story-line; and a good producer will have the eye and
the touch of a good editor. The director has to make
everything work in front of the camera, has to believe in
the characters and their situations and persuade everyone
else to believe in them, too.

It is a pleasure to acknowledge wholeheartedly the parts
played by my producers and director in the writing of this
serial: and I am sure, by the time I see it, that I shall be
equally grateful to a talented cast for bringing it all to life.

The first idea for *The Country Boy* came when my wife
and I were on holiday in France. We were deep in the
beautiful countryside of the Auvergne, hearing no earthly
sounds on our walks but cow bells and streams running
down into the valleys. There were no cars, no aeroplanes,
not even a trace of vapour trail in the blue sky. And as we
enjoyed all this, we thought of some of the children we
teach back in noisy, crowded London, and we were moved

by how lucky we were to be there in the country for a break. I began to think about a child transformed the other way, from country to alien town, and the effects such an enforced change might have.

When I had the chance, I talked about it to Paul Stone, the producer at the BBC with whom I had worked on *Running Scared*. There would be no money for filming in France! That was said straight away, although he liked the story possibilities. Later, when I was seeking a peaceful spot in the sun to write up some notes, my car somehow took me back to the Kent marshes of Dickens and *Great Expectations*, an area in which I had once lived. And suddenly the Auvergne became the Cliffe Marshes, not beautiful countryside but remote-feeling and moody terrain down by the Thames – and Paul Stone decided that he could film it there, on location.

The locations used in the serial are those I had in my head from actually seeing them: the unique barn-like look of Boatrick House, which became the Westcotts' farm, and a line of disused coastguards' houses (according to the Ordnance Survey map) which became my villains' hiding place. The BBC went further and even built a shack for old Alice on a small estuary island, with everything complete inside for interior filming.

Paul Stone retired from the BBC during the writing of the serial and Brenda Ennis, an independent producer, came in to see the project through. She encouraged me to go back to writing the simple, straightforward story of the country boy, Ben, and his family, taking time to develop him and to like him instead of some of the 'snappy' television scenes I had produced. A novel on film, she asked for. But that, when written, was over-stretched at two and a half hours, and more adventurous excitement was called for. At this point Colin Cant joined the partnership as director, and remembered elements of my first draft for Paul Stone which he had liked very much and thought should return. So they did; and now we had a story operating at two levels – that of the country boy, and that thriller element coming from the smugglers whose water he stirs.

There aren't too many technical details in these scripts, which are those used by the actors; they are not those technical marked-up scripts which Colin Cant draws up, showing camera angles, cuts, dissolves, fades, and all the jargon of the effects. We may still need to know whether it's day or night, interior or exterior: otherwise, the only abbreviation I use is the occasional (*oov.*) – *out of vision* (sounds or voices off-camera). In other respects scripts read like fast-moving stories: the guts of what happens; and I hope there is some pleasure in reading this one.

Bernard Ashley
August, 1988

The series was shot on location between 5th September and 11th November 1988.

EPISODE ONE

A fishing launch in the river, night

Scot and Brit, two tough S.A.S. imitations, are on board heading down river towards a rendezvous. Ted, the boat's middle-aged skipper from Chatham, is at the helm. We hear the puttering of another engine, see some lights.

SCOT.   Who's that?

BRIT.   'S not them.

Brit picks up a fishing rod. The other boat approaches. Muffled, from its cabin, we hear three or four cockney voices singing 'My Way'. The boat passes on the right side.

SKIPPER.   *From the other boat.* You going out?

SCOT.   Aye. Bitin', are they?

SKIPPER.   Dunno. Only blinkin' fish I've got are human.

'My Way' comes to its impossible climax.

SKIPPER.   Got stopped twice so they started on the booze.

BRIT.   Stopped?

SKIPPER.   Coastguard playing silly devils.

SCOT.   Oh, aye? What, drugs an' that, is it?

SKIPPER.   Dunno. Frightening the fish, I know that.

The other boat goes.

TED.   That's all we needed.

BRIT.   No, don't jump; he could be up to some con. Keep on for a bit.

The launch – in the estuary

There is no moon. The launch is going forward at half speed. Ted, Scot and Brit looking out cautiously.

TED.   See anything?

SCOT.   A fair drop o' stuff you canna' drink.

BRIT.   We on course?

TED.   *Thumps his binnacle.* Yeah, we'll see 'em if they're there.

BRIT.   They will be! *He looks at his watch.*

A sudden searchlight sweeps across the water a few metres short of the boat.

TED.   Bloody Nora! *He spins the wheel about and revs up.*

BRIT.   Coastguard! Give it some!

BRIT.   *To Ted.* Come on, move it!

The searchlight sweeps and flares into the camera.

The marshes near Egypt Creek

General view of the marshes and the river, setting us in the flat landscape where the tallest intrusion into the sky is a burn-off chimney at the oil refinery on the far side of the Thames. The sky itself is full of false light, the last of the brightness before the rain. It is about seven o'clock on a summer evening. We come in on Alice and Ben, her grandson, picking herbs and flowers along the the edge of a straight dyke, near to the sea wall. Duke, the Westcotts' collie dog, is with them, mostly sniffing out his own interests but coming back to Ben from time to time for approval. Meanwhile Alice's dog, Jem, a younger brother of Duke and much more skittish, is everywhere. Ben is a boy of about twelve, small for his age and you somehow

*think of him as wearing glasses, although he doesn't. He is
in jeans and a tee-shirt, with wellingtons. Alice is about
sixty-five, dark-skinned from exposure to the country life.
She is in a tee-shirt, too, unironed and stained with old
fruits but clean. She wears this outside a pair of
comfortable patched trousers, which are tucked inside stout
boots with a show of thick sock. On her left hand, with
which she roots and grasps, is an old leather glove. She
hasn't had the right hand for some years. Over her
shoulder is a large bag made from an old curtain in which
she puts what she picks. She is tall, with her hair up and
falling out of combs. Alice and Ben are clearly after a
special plant today; there is a lot of looking and not much
picking.*

BEN.   *Eagerly, staring at a leaf and holding it up.* Is this
one?

ALICE.   *Without looking up.* No.

BEN.   *Sniffs it, lets it drop.* Thought not.

ALICE.   Wrong side of the dyke.

*They search on contentedly, no need for words. Looking
up, Ben can't see Duke. He looks around then whistles
him. Duke comes running along the dyke's edge.*

BEN.   Good boy. *He pats him and goes on.*

*Alice has caught up with Ben as he picks another leaf.
Wordlessly he shows it to her.*

ALICE.   *Nods.* Now, take half, leave half.

*Ben stoops to do so, but it has been a back-aching couple
of hours.*

BEN.   Your back all right, Nan?

ALICE.   Not felt it in fifty years.

She roots on with agility.

Alice's house, early evening

*Alice lives on the margin between the marsh and the sea,
near to the sea wall. Her house is a small and ancient
timber building with a corrugated roof, mossed over. There
is a privy away from the house and a wood-store of sawn
and stacked driftwood and river timbers nearby. Chickens
roam free, and in and out of Jem's kennel. Alice's shack is
on a small island reached by a frail wooden bridge. A bed
of herbs grows near the door. The sky is looking more
threatening now, but only with rain, it won't be a thunder
storm. Duke runs into shot first, followed by Jem, yapping
around him. Ben and Alice approach, Ben now carrying
Alice's bag of herbs, she with an arm around his shoulder.
They are singing and stepping out.*

BEN AND ALICE.   "The grand old Duke of York,
He had ten thousand men,
He marched them up to the top of the hill,
And he marched them down again."

ALICE.   *As they go into the house.* Daft 'ap'orth, weren't
he?

Ben laughs.

Alice's house – the room, early evening

*This is the only room to the house. A simple bed with a
truckle beneath it is against one wall, the sink is old and
high and square, there is a wood stove, and rows and rows
of bottles and jars, all labelled. There is no television, no
telephone, but a very old radio. Ben and Alice are up at
the table in the middle of the room. Ben has a small
chopping board and a sharp knife. He is chopping the
plant leaves like mint. Alice is picking whole washed leaves
from a muslin cloth, which she has dried, lettuce-style, by
twirling. When she is satisfied that the leaves are good, she
drops them onto Ben's chopping board. When his board is
full, Ben scoops the chopped leaves into a large jar, then*

begins again. Alice, having finished her part of the job, goes to a drawer for a roll of small freezer bags and ties. She waits while Ben finishes chopping, then scoops the last of the leaves into one.

BEN. Freezer bags?

Alice hunches her shoulders to acknowledge the anomaly with humour. She takes the tied bag to the windowsill and places it among others like a prescription awaiting collection at the chemist.

ALICE. *She looks out at the weather.* Better get off now, mister, you got no mac.

BEN. Oh! Not yet!

ALICE. Yes, yet. Come again soon.

Alice goes to a cupboard and takes out a home-baked loaf. Turning the herb cutting board over, she slices him off a crust.

ALICE. Here y'are.

BEN. Oooh. *He gets up, sniffs the crust, starts on it.* Co-op!

ALICE. *Swipes at him playfully.* I'll give you Co-op!

From a hook on the wall she unwinds a small sewn bag from among others; it contains scented herbs. She gives it to Ben.

Here.

Ben frowns.

ALICE. For Mum's sweet dreams.

Ben sniffs it, puts it in his pocket.

BEN. Cheers. Better'n smelling Dad. Ta-ta, Nan.

ALICE. Ta-ta, mister. Go on with you.

Ben goes out.

BEN.   Come on, Duke. Good boy.

Alice follows him to the door. Duke and Jem bark.

Outside Alice's house, early evening

It is darker now and rain is imminent. Ben, eating his crust, cycles off on an old bike, Duke and Jem running to him, but Jem falling back and returning. Ben turns and waves to Alice in the doorway.

ALICE.   Love to Dad and everyone.

BEN.   Yeah. See you, Nan. *He looks up as the first spots fall.*

ALICE.   Here!

She goes in and comes out again with a sack, which she runs to give him.

Go on! Dodge the drops!

She watches him cycling off.

To Jem.   Come on, then.

She takes him inside and shuts the door.

The Old Customs Houses – roadway, early evening

It is raining steadily now. Dodging the pot-holes in the unmade road, Ben cycles past the houses on his way home, Duke at his side.

The Old Customs Houses – downstairs room, early evening

Brit and Scot are preparing to leave the derelict house. One sleeping roll has been set by the door, Brit is rolling the other. By the window, Scot is clearing an upturned box of sugar packet, mugs, etc.   (oov.) Duke barks.

BRIT.   *In a voice too loud for Scot.* You ready?

SCOT.   Shut it! *He looks out of the window.* There's a snottie an' a dog!

BRIT.   Eh? *He runs out of the room and up the stairs.*

The Old Customs Houses – upstairs room, early evening

The room is bare with peeling paper and mould on the walls – except in one corner where a tarpaulin covers a pile of hidden canisters. Brit runs into the room and looks through the window, standing back behind the light line, SAS style. We see Ben and Duke heading inland for home, the inlet in the background. Satisfied, Brit turns away. As he makes to go back downstairs, his foot catches the rope handle at the corner of the tarpaulin, pulling the cover off the ten stacked canisters. We see them fairly clearly, each sealed with a yellow 'Toxic' tape marked 'J.M.C. D22' all the way round.

BRIT.   *Disentangling his foot.* Get off!

He replaces the tarpaulin and goes downstairs.

Westcotts' farmhouse, evening

This is house and barn built as one, the house at the front. It is unique in design, almost like an upturned ark. Outside is Duke's kennel, Dave's old Volvo, Lyn's egg-round van, and a few wandering chickens – the real egg business is battery. A downstairs light shines from the kitchen at the side. It is evening not night, but in the rain the light shows up. Ben and Duke cycle and run towards the house.

Westcotts' farmhouse – kitchen, evening

The kitchen looks 1930's suburban rather than stereotyped 'farmhouse'. The usual appliances are there but the cupboards are of real wood, painted white or cream. Lyn,

Ben's mother, who is attractive and in singlet and jeans, is at the draining board transferring eggs from battered trays of twenty-four into half-dozen boxes. She has a bowl of water and a saucer of soil in front of her. Every so often she dips an egg into the water and touches it in the soil. As she closes one of the small boxes we can see why. It has 'Direct from the farm' printed on it. Sally, fifteen and very happy about something, is peeling potatoes dreamily, cutting off as much as she leaves. We watch the egg packing. On the third box, Lyn takes a downy feather from a previously unseen dish of feathers and sticks it to an egg with water. Sally goes to plop a potato into the saucepan but she misses. An arrival bark from Duke heralds Ben's entrance. He comes in with the sack over his head, like a farmhand. Duke has stayed outside in his kennel.

BEN.   Bloomin' wet!

LYN.   Rain is. Feet! *Sees the sack.* And put that out.

Ben throws the sack out of the back door. He looks at the stove, into the saucepan, crowding Lyn as he passes.

BEN.   What's for tea?

LYN.   Omelettes, you make me drop one of these.

Ben makes to go on through but he remembers Alice's perfumed sachet.

BEN.   *Gives it to Lyn.* From Nan. She said, "Sweet dreams."

LYN.   *Not taking it, leaving Ben to put it on the draining board.* Oh, yes?

Ben goes into the house and comes back with a rough towel for Duke.

LYN.   *Throws the sachet onto a shelf.* Hope your dad's not long. It's a dirty old night.

SALLY.   *Dreamily*. Is it?

Lyn sees how poorly Sally is doing. Exasperated, she takes the knife and potato from her to do it herself.

BEN.   *Going out to Duke*. To-ny!

SALLY.   *Blushing*. What you on about?

Lyn gives Sally a knowing look.

The Old Customs Houses, night

The Land Rover is parked outside, Brit at the wheel. Scot emerges from the houses and runs through the rain to throw two bedding rolls into the vehicle. He bangs on the side and jumps up into the back. Without lights, the Land Rover drives off inland, avoiding the pot-holes as Ben had done.

The gateway to a field, night.

It is raining quite heavily now. Dave, Ben's father, is finishing the urgent repair of a gate catch with Henry, his old and toothless casual hand. Dave is in his mid-thirties, a country man who thinks long and looks hard before speaking: but when he does speak, people take notice. He is bare-headed but in an old fawn raincoat tied with rope. Dave tries the gate several times, is not dis-satisfied, but he says nothing. He sees the Land Rover bumping past and watches it with hard eyes.

Ben's field

It is about seven o'clock in a clear field with sheep hurdles arranged in an open-ended box with a gate. Ben is working alone with Duke (there are no sheep), on a bright summer morning. Ben gives Duke commands, "Come by", "Lay down, Duke", giving a series of whistles which send him running left or right. The sequence ends with Ben crouching to Duke, congratulating him with pats on the head.

BEN.   Good boy. Good old boy. Champion!

Duke breaks from the sheep dog mould and licks Ben's face excitedly, knocking him over backwards in the wet grass.

BEN.   Oi! *But he laughs as Duke licks him some more.*

Dave, still in his raincoat, comes up on them.

DAVE.   Don't you give him too much of that.

BEN.   What?

DAVE.   Lovey-dovey. He's got to do a day's work for me when you've gone to school.

Ben pushes Duke away. Duke runs over and lays at Dave's feet. Ben gets up.

BEN.   What you reckon? You seen us?

DAVE.   Grammar. "Did you see us?" Looks like you're coming on with him.

BEN.   He still won't answer me, not always.

DAVE.   He's a sheep dog, i'n't he? Got to use his head, got to use it when you're not using yours. Times he can't see you and you can't see him – way over the back fields – how you gonna tell him what to do? How do you know what he's got to do?

Ben shrugs.

DAVE.   Well, then. Never mind the blessed East Kent. Show's one thing, working's another. *Looks at the sun.* Come on! Breakfast.

BEN.   I'll be all right. Got a lot to do.

DAVE.   So's he. Breakfast.

Dave goes off. Duke stays, gets up and comes to Ben who gives him a secret pat.

BEN.   Good boy. Good old Duke. Gonna win, eh? Gonna win!

Ben pushes Duke off, who runs to catch up with Dave, striding away.

Country road leading into Littlechurch

Ben and Sally on board. A single-decker school bus winds its way from the farms to one of the built-up estates outside Rochester.

The School Bus

The bus is driving towards the school. Sally is looking fresh and pretty, still full of the joys of spring, although her face is set so as not to give too much away to the dozen or so other children from the farms and villages. Ben, by contrast, just about made it to the bus and is still buttoning his school shirt under his tie.

Littlechurch Secondary School – classroom

This is the English room on the first floor with a view of the marshes and the river. Ben is at a desk by the window, which is open. He is staring out, his mind more out of the room than in it. The rest of the class are looking at him, waiting.

VARIOUS PUPILS.   Come on, Westcott! It's easy, man. Oh, tell him, someone.

MRS. CRADDOCK.   Yes, we'd all like to be out there, Ben. But we most certainly shan't go home till you answer the question.

Ben has come back to them, but he is lost.

MRS. CRADDOCK.   I sometimes think I'd do better with
you if I communicated by whistles. But poetry, I'm
afraid, is the stuff of words. *With a resigned patience.*

"Here rests his head upon the lap of earth.
A youth to Fortune and to Fame unknown ..."

She looks round to the others.

VARIOUS PUPILS.   Gray's Elegy.

'Elegy Written in a Country Churchyard'.

Down your way, i'n it? Bloomin' easy!

MRS. CRADDOCK.   Indeed! "Bloomin' easy"! Eh, Ben?

BEN.   Yes, Miss. Hold on. *He stares ahead and recites.*
"Fair Science frowned not on his humble birth,
And Melancholy marked him for her own,
Large was his bounty –"

MRS. CRADDOCK.   Oh! Well, then! Most impressive.

Ben gets a round of applause from the rest of the class.

BEN.   *Bowing.* Cheers, fans.

MRS. CRADDOCK.   Now shut the window, please – and
we'll all homeward plod our weary ways ...

BEN.   An' cheers, Gel.

*We see where Ben has recited from – Gerry's propped-up
book on the desk in front. Gerry gathers it up as Ben shuts
the window and joins in the rush to the door.*

Littlechurch Secondary School – girls' toilets

*Sounds of children leaving the school building. Sally is in
front of one of the mirrors putting a touch of make-up to
her eyes. She is aware of the door. Jo and Lisa are
watching her with amusement, Jo leaning on a lavatory
door, chewing.*

JO.   Hope he goes for all this heavy stuff.

LISA.   Watch it don't go in your eye.

SALLY.   Just watch the door. I know what I'm doing.

JO.   My mum'd kill me.

SALLY.   After me, if you don't watch that door.

(oov.) A bus horn.

LISA.   Come on, your bus'll go.

JO.   He'll think you've cancelled him.

SALLY.   *Last rushed check.* He's not a bloomin' concert!

Littlechurch Secondary School – the road

The three girls run out. Jo and Lisa stop running and walk off towards the estate. Sally runs towards the School Bus. Ben is in the seat by the door. There are perhaps ten other children in the vehicle.

BEN.   *Out of the door, going to hurry her, but notices her make-up.* Are you sure?

Sally gives him a look, gets in, slides the bus door shut and the vehicles pulls away.

The School Bus

The bus is driving out towards the marshes. Most of the children are chattering to one another, but Ben is contentedly alone, staring out above the hedges. Idly, he looks at his name in the paper, listed for the sheep dog trials. Sally is also on her own, dabbing on some perfume. A first-form boy watches her, fascinated. Sally sits up and takes in some deep breaths. She forces out a stare at the first-former, but it isn't unfriendly: she knows she looks good. We hear the roar of motor-bikes. A gang of three youths on noisy machines overtake the bus. They have the

*'biker' look of rough country youth about them: long hair,
leather waistcoats and chains – old-fashioned. As the bikes
overtake, one of the youths spots Sally and leers. She looks
away haughtily, then smiles to herself.*

Top of the escarpment – end of the road

*The bus stops. Ben and Sally get out. Ben stands and
draws in the country air, visibly relaxes.*

SALLY.   Tell Mum I won't be long. I'm –

BEN.   Rollin' in the long grass!

SALLY.   Jealous!

Ben puckers up and does her a long, noisy kiss.

BEN.   See you.

SALLY.   You get more like your dog every day.

*Ben walks on down the track. The bus reverses and drives
away. Sally watches it, then slowly follows Ben down the
track.*

Track leading down to the marshes, day

*Ben comes to a turn in the track, the marshes and the
river beyond, fields of sheep and the inlet. Ben takes a
deliberate stance, looking down towards the bushes
overhanging the water. He puts his fingers in his mouth
and gives the 'Come by me' whistle. Duke breaks cover
and runs towards Ben.*

BEN.   Good boy. Good Duke. Good old boy.

Ben and Duke greet each other.

BEN.   Done with Dad? Done your work? We gonna win
that cup, then? Your name's in the paper! Eh? Gonna
read it? *He gives the rolled-up paper to Duke.* Come on,
boy. Good Duke. Come on, stay by.

Ben walks towards home, turning right at the foot of the track: Duke with him, delighted but disciplined, dropping the paper.

BEN.   Don't you like your name in the paper? *Picks it up.* Come on, then.

Footpath to J.M. Chemicals (UK) Ltd.

The foot of the escarpment. Geographically, this footpath leads to the front gate of J.M. Chemicals. *A metalled, major road also leads in – the main route to the site. Sally is coming down the track from where the bus dropped her. She can go right, where Ben has gone towards home, or left. She goes left beneath a sign reading* 'Footpath to J.M. Chemicals (UK) Limited only. No public right of way'. *The sign has been peppered with shotgun pellets. Sally's face lights up as she sees someone coming. A quick hand goes to the neck of her shirt. We see Tony approaching on his bike. On the bike's pannier is a plastic bag with homework in it, beneath a folded blazer. Tony, a sixth-former from Gravesend Grammar School, is in a white shirt, the tie removed like Sally's.*

SALLY.   Watch out!

Tony cycles up to her. She holds his handlebars.

TONY.   Watch out for what?

SALLY.   You could've come off.

Sally lets go of his handlebars and he does a long controlled wobble, straight at her. She jumps back.

SALLY.   Watch out!

TONY.   Perfect control. Was your bus late?

SALLY.   A bit. *Stares at him innocently.* Slow getting away. *They start to walk off.* And I mustn't be too long.

Bank of the inlet – near the Old Customs Houses

Tony and Sally come in through some bushes.

TONY.   Wanna swim?

Sally stares at him. This has implications.

SALLY.   *Breaks the mood.* My dad'd kill me if I went in there.

TONY.   Why? Is it dangerous?

SALLY.   He reckons. River comes in, currents. He's real strict about it.

Tony puts his hand up to her to sit down, but we hear the sound of the bikers approaching.

SALLY.   Oh, no!

TONY.   Them again!

SALLY.   Come on.

They run out onto the road to be in the open when the bikers get there.

The inlet

The three bikers come along the track to the Customs Houses, forming into a circle around Sally and Tony, who try to look tolerantly amused. This mustn't be too menacing, the ad libs more to do with biking skill than menace.

The Old Customs Houses

They park up their bikes.

BAZ.   'Old on! Gotta go somewhere.

OTHERS.   Yah! Yeah!

Baz runs to the house Brit and Scot have been in. We hear splintering wood.

DIV.   What we gonna do?

PILK.   You busted all the windows.

Baz opens the upstairs windows of the house.

BAZ.   'Ere, look! *He lifts a canister in his hands.* Targets!

DIV.   Better than nothing.

BAZ.   Some old farmer's fertilizer! *Slings it down from window.*

Bank of the inlet

The canister is standing on a post at the inlet's edge. The three youths are throwing flints at it. Div takes aim. He just pings it.

PILK.   Only clipped it.

DIV.   Rotten shot.

Pilk throws. There is a dull clunk.

PILK.   Boom! Oh, yes!

DIV.   Smackeroo!

BAZ.   *Picks up a bigger flint.* Watch this! Top third, in the 'ead, smack it over. *He takes very careful aim, throws, misses.*

PILK.   Yah! Missed it!

DIV.   Oh, smack it over! Wallie!

Baz, enraged, jumps up, runs to the canister and throws it into the inlet.

BAZ.   Smack in! All right?

Close up of the canister sinking, one small flint hole sending out a first fine curl of yellow chemical.

J.M. Chemicals (UK) Ltd

Establishing shot of J.M. Chemicals (UK) Limited.

Dr. Skellman's laboratory

An empty canister of D22 *stands on the workbench, which is beneath a large window looking out onto the marshes and the river, clearly setting* J.M. Chemicals *in the locality we've been in already. The room is about the size of a school classroom, set up with various tubes and retorts. There are refrigerators, sinks and work surfaces. Lesley Skellman is twenty-nine, attractive but not in a striking way – it's more subtle than that. Her skin, her pale eyes and her soft blonde hair give her an almost transparent effect – in contrast to the tough cookie she really is. Wearing a pair of surgical gloves, she is spinning a yellow chemical in a centrifuge which has an electronic read-out. She is noting the latest of a series of results. Stephen West comes in – a twenty-nine-year-old university whizz-kid, wearing a tie but with the top button of his shirt undone to show how active he is.*

WEST.   How's it going, Les?

DR. SKELLMAN.   *Finishes making an entry.* Did you knock? Please knock in future.

WEST.   What progress? Is the stuff safe yet?

DR. SKELLMAN.   I could dilute it tomorrow but you want something else!

WEST.   I want something cost effective.

DR. SKELLMAN.   Separating molecules takes time.

WEST.   Time is what we haven't got.

He goes quickly, without giving her the option not to reply to him.

The laboratory annexe

In a small hot corner, dressed for the summer in a loose black singlet and Bermuda shorts, Charmaine is at the computer. Her taste in hair and make-up is extreme, her nails like long blue talons on the keyboard. She is very bright: not pleased at present. Stephen West goes past, coming out of the laboratory. West looks at her but she doesn't want to see him. He goes on out. After tapping one more entry, Charmaine looks happier.

DR. SKELLMAN.   *(oov.)* Charmaine!

CHARMAINE.   Yes, Les. *She goes to the laboratory door. We can see Dr. Skellman from here.*

DR. SKELLMAN.   I'm out of D.22. You couldn't . . .

CHARMAINE.   Sure. What are computer whizz-kids for?

Dr. Skellman smiles and goes back to her centrifuge. Charmaine takes some industrial gloves from her drawer and goes out to the warehouse.

J.M. Chemicals – the warehouse

The warehouse is filled with stacked cartons, crates, etc, a fork-lift truck and wooden pallets of pharmaceuticals. At one end of the warehouse stands a caged area housing rows of shining canisters of the sort already seen. Charmaine comes to the sliding door of the bonded cage. She taps a combination on the electronic lock, slides the door and goes inside. She drags a set of industrial steps to the canisters and climbs to the first accessible row – at the front top. She is about to lift the end canister off when she looks carefully at the spacing of the row. She leans back to compare it with other rows. There is something wrong. Charmaine's frown asks 'Who's been messing around?' She temporarily replaces the end canister and starts to count the row.

Ben's field

*A burning sun shows how hot it is. A long shot shows the
oil refinery shimmering in the heat. Pull back and drop to
where Ben is working with Duke and a group of eight
sheep. They are going through trialling manoeuvres, and
we should care whether dog and boy can pen the sheep.
The work is good and the sheep are penned, with Ben
letting the gate shut on its rope. He is very hot.*

A large field of sheep

*Ben and Duke drive the group of sheep back into the field
with the others.*

BEN.   Good boy, Duke. Good boy!

Ben closes the gate and leans on it, perspiring.

BEN.   Phew!

*He wipes his face on his shirt. We see Duke panting. Ben
has a thought and looks all around cautiously.*

BEN.   Come on, boy. Come on!

Crouching, Ben runs towards some trees, Duke with him.

The track by the Old Customs Houses

*Ben comes to the track on the side away from the inlet.
Furtively, he looks up and down the track and whistles.
Duke comes out of cover and runs across to the bushes by
the inlet. After a second look to see that it's clear, Ben
runs crouching across into the bushes, too.*

The inlet's edge

*This is where Sally and Tony were, and the bikers. Ben
comes from the bushes to the water's edge. He is followed
by Duke. Ben realises that he has his watch on. He puts it
on the post where the canister was for target practice.*

*After a careful look around, Ben dives into the water.
Duke plunges in after him.*

The inlet – under water

*Ben dives into fairly clear water. It all looks cool and
refreshing. As Ben surfaces, though, we stay under and
descend a foot or so to the inlet bed where the kicked
canister can be seen still oozing yellow poison into the
water. It is coming thicker now.*

The inlet – surface

Ben and Duke are playing in the water. Ben laughs.

BEN.   Why do dogs only do dog paddle? Eh?

*Looking up, Ben sees Dave driving his old Volvo along the
track.*

BEN.   Oh, no! Dad!

*The car stops and Dave looks round. Ben's face shows how
scared he is of being seen by Dave.*

BEN.   Down boy, under!

He grabs Duke's collar and pulls him under.

The inlet – under water

*Ben descends into the deeper yellowish water. In a panic to
get up Duke swallows water and fights with Ben, which
makes him swallow water, too, before kicking wildly for the
surface.*

The inlet's edge

*Ben surfaces to see Dave's car disappear. He struggles for
the bank and pulls himself out of the water, grabbing at his
watch. He spits and coughs as he looks up and down in the
water and on the bank for Duke, of whom there is no sign.*

BEN.   Duke! Good ... Duke! Duke!

Ben goes on searching the water and the bank, looking very worried.

END OF EPISODE ONE

EPISODE TWO

Ben's field

Ben is looking for Duke. His hair has dried from his swim. (oov.): A car hooter. Ben sees his father's car coming. Dave leans his head out of the car.

DAVE.   Ben!

BEN.   *Coughs.* Dad . . .

DAVE.   Come on! Nan's. Where's that dog?

BEN.   He's . . . gone off somewhere.

DAVE.   Too easy with him!

Impatiently, he opens the car door.

BEN.   Dad! He's . . . *He can't say it – just indicates that he's gone.*

DAVE.   Off chasing rabbits. Looked all over for you. Trials! Got to think of something else sometimes.

Ben looks round for Duke again.

DAVE.   Come on then! Thought you liked getting out to Nan's.

BEN.   But Duke . . .

DAVE.   Don't be soft. Get in.

Reluctantly, Ben gets in.

DAVE.   He'll be back home by now.

The car drives off.

The inlet – an overhung bank

Duke, bedraggled, wretched and whining, pulls himself out of the water and crawls away into the bushes.

Way to Egypt Creek – road and lane junction

Dave's car turns off an 'A' road onto a single track lane. The purpose in showing this is to establish that Westcotts' farm is a car drive away from Alice's house – even though Ben often chooses to walk or cycle it. As the car passes, Ben, with his window down, is still looking all round for Duke, on the off-chance.

Dave's car

Dave and Ben are in the car, Ben still looking out, Dave taking glances at him, puzzled.

DAVE.   What's up with you?

Ben shakes his head.

DAVE.   Mind those branches.

Alice's house

Jem barks around their feet as Dave's car arrives with a single toot. Alice comes out of the house eagerly, and for a second we see her pleasure; but by the time the car door slams she has recovered a matter-of-fact almost aggressive stance

ALICE.   And what have you two come disturbing my peace for?

DAVE.   *Getting out, softer with this dominant woman.* Come to see you're behaving yourself.

ALICE.   Ha! Haven't been tempted in twenty years. And my Ben!

BEN.   'Lo, Nan.

Alice hugs him but the squeeze makes him cough.

ALICE.   What's the matter, mister? *She holds him at arm's length.* This ain't the boy over here Monday. What's up? What's up with you, then?

DAVE.   Cough in the summer!

BEN.   It's Duke.

DAVE.   Yeah, lost the run of the dog.

ALICE.   Oh, he'll be all right. But you don't look the ticket for a fine day. Skin like a candle, you got there, mister . . .

Ben catches his breath at being the centre of all this attention – and coughs again.

ALICE.   Like a hedgehog in your throat?

Ben nods.

ALICE.   Baked hedgehog? Hot?

Ben nods again.

ALICE.   Let's see what I've got for that.

They go inside.

Alice's house – the room

Alice has brought a kettle to boil on the stove. She pokes the fire to keep it going while she lifts down a jar from a shelf and unscrews the lid. Ben is sitting in a chair. Dave watches from the doorway.

ALICE.   Now then – very good for a cough, this is. *Primula Veris.* Cowslip.

BEN.   *Holding his stomach now.* I'll be all right. Got all hot, that's all . . .

Alice takes some dried petals from the jar, chops them and puts them into an infuser. She stirs it vigorously and pours the liquid into a mug for drinking.

ALICE.   Now, every last drop.

Ben drinks.

ALICE.   There! You've tasted worse. Now you'll feel it starting to work.

Dave comes in from the doorway.

DAVE.   *Sniffing the jar.* Huh! Remember this!

Ben puts the mug down with a bang.

ALICE.   All gone? *She feels his damp head.* What's up with you, eh? Getting ill in the summer?

A Middle-Eastern Embassy

In a London square, narrow and run-down, a brass plate at the door says 'Embassy' in Arabic. A policeman stands at the door, doing his duty without acknowledging any of the comings and goings. A large white Mercedes is parked outside. The Embassy door opens and the chauffeur, a young man in a dark suit and an open-necked shirt, comes round to the rear door of the car. Mr. Martouf comes out – about forty, slim and fit with ungiving eyes. His suit is white, more expensive, and his open-necked shirt is made of silk. He gets into the Merc, which drives away watched by the policeman. The camera rises to a dormer window. A net curtain falls into place as if someone has been watching. The light in the room goes off. Cut to the front door. Iraj Asfia, a young man of student age, dressed in a collarless shirt and light trousers, comes out of the building.

IRAJ.   *To the policeman.* Good evening.

He hurries off down the pavement watched by the silent policeman.

A phone booth

Iraj hurries through the crowds to an empty phone.

'The News' office at Wapping

A large, modern, open-plan newspaper office, not nearly as dramatic as old films suggest. Along a wall the golden words "'The News' – all day, morning, noon and night" tell us where we are. Adam Roberts, a young, sharp, reporter in red glasses is sitting at one side of a double desk, Bill Podger, an older journalist, opposite him. Each has a computer keyboard and a screen. A phone rings near him.

BILL.   News desk. Yes, speaking. *He cups the phone and shouts to Adam.* Our Embassy friend again.

Adam looks up, then carries on.

BILL.   Yeah, go on . . . .

A phone booth

Iraj is talking anxiously into the phone. A meeting is being set up. Reluctantly he nods to the only meeting place Bill Podger will give him. He looks round nervously again, puts the phone down, and hurries away.

'The News' office at Wapping

BILL.   *Putting his phone down.* Who's our Middle East expert?

ADAM.   Cyril. You sent him to Iceland.

BILL.   What do you know about the Middle East?

ADAM.   It's hot. And dangerous.

Side of Westcotts' farmhouse

Lyn is sweeping out her egg van. Sally is on a cheap sun-bed in a bikini, wearing a Walkman and reading a

*simplified French novel for homework. She has a small
dictionary with her. We can hear the tinny rhythm from
the Walkman.*

LYN.   Sal, turn that down, will you?

*Sally doesn't hear. Lyn goes over and turns it down
herself.*

LYN.   Rather hear it properly.

Sally takes it off.

SALLY.   Bloomin' French!

LYN.   I could do with such hard work!

SALLY.   *Throws the book down.* Always police stuff! Why
can't they give us something else? *She looks up a word
in her dictionary.*

LYN.   *Leaning on her broom.* What? Love, romance?

SALLY.   *Uneasy.* Do worse! But this . . .

LYN.   *Leans against the van, folds her arms.* What's his
name?

SALLY.   *Picks up the book.* Claude Chaumet. *But she has
understood Lyn's tone.* Tony. He's ever so nice . . .

LYN.   He'd have to be. How old?

SALLY.   I think he's . . . in the sixth form . . . Gravesend
Grammar.

LYN.   *Brushing at a difficult corner.* Upper sixth or lower
sixth?

SALLY.   Um, upper . . . Yeah, upper.

LYN.   He's eighteen then. *Stops again.* A man . . .

Sally hitches up her bikini top.

SALLY.   He's still at school . . .

LYN.   So are you, love. *Refers to the homework.* With a good way to go.

Lyn smiles, is going to give some good advice but thinks better of it, goes back to her sweeping.

A tourist spot

At a café table, Bill and Iraj have met. Iraj is nervous, swallows a Coke down quickly.

BILL.   Had to meet you, old man. Got to know you're not a hoax.

IRAJ.   A hoax! I'm risking my life. *Looks all around again.*

BILL.   So what's the strength? What do you want with us?

IRAJ.   To open people's eyes, stop supplies. In our war they're using chemical bombs – along the border, on people who used to be our cousins. Killing everyone, old people, women, children.

BILL.   Yeah, it's a dirty business, war. But –

IRAJ.   A dirty business. Oh, yes. And dirty business people making the chemical. British business people.

BILL.   Ah! You're saying it's going out from Britain?

IRAJ.   *Politely exasperated.* This is why I'm talking to you. Over to France, down to Marseilles, across the Mediterranean.

BILL.   Be a good story – but I've got no proof, have I? We upset a foreign government we've got to have proof . . .

IRAJ.   Go out there. See my cousins dying.

BILL.   Oh, I believe out there. I want proof –

IRAJ.   Here? You're the newspaper. Investigate. Please! I'm as good as dead already.

The road to Westcotts' farm

*Ben and Dave coming back from their search for Duke.
But the real indication of who it is is the sound of Ben's
infrequent coughing. It is a dry cough, although Ben's
main pain is in his stomach.*

Side of Westcotts' farmhouse

*Duke's kennel is near the back door. Ben hurries to it,
followed by Dave. But it is empty, just an old car rug in
there. Ben turns away. He knows miracles don't happen —
he drowned Duke. Lyn opens the kitchen door, stands and
looks. Head down, Ben goes past her into the house.*

DAVE.   Stupid dog! Hard work without.

A clump of dyke bushes near the sea wall

*We can hear some river sounds at first, the distant hooter
of a ship, then the sound of Duke coughing. A close-up of
the distressed dog shows him lying down; but with an effort
he stands and drags himself off.*

Dr. Skellman's garden

*A small cottage garden, sweet peas and a tiny lawn, where
Lesley Skellman is on her own, watering plants in the
shade with an old-fashioned watering can. She is dressed
almost lacily in white, like the pale Englishwoman in
India. Charmaine, colourful and modern, comes in through
a side gate carrying two large cartons of milk shake.*

CHARMAINE.   *Calling as she comes.* Knock, knock! Your
servant didn't answer the door . . .

DR. SKELLMAN.   Got the day off. Come to help me in the
garden?

CHARMAINE.   Do square wheels roll? No way! Here —
build you up. *She gives Lesley a milk shake.* Got a
minute? Course you have.

DR. SKELLMAN.   What's this?

CHARMAINE.   Milk shake.

DR. SKELLMAN.   What's in it?

CHARMAINE.   Milk . . . and shake.

Lesley Skellman tries it gingerly.

DR. SKELLMAN.   My mother would turn in her grave.

CHARMAINE.   She's not dead.

DR. SKELLMAN.   It'd kill her. *Sips.* You didn't come out from Chatham for this?

CHARMAINE.   Les – I'm worried, I've got to talk, right? I can't stop trying to figure it. Those canisters. Killer-diller. We're ten short! That's not counting what you've used for tests. Five hundred litres of embargoed stuff that mustn't be shifted.

DR. SKELLMAN.   *Lightly.* Yes, you said.

CHARMAINE.   I've thought of nothing else. Been going round and round. And who holds the combination of the cage apart from Wonder-girl? Westie! And Sir Double-barrelled Double-barrelled. Blow the risk, sneak it out the back door and make the dosh. That's all they care.

DR. SKELLMAN.   *Getting more water.* Hold on! Where are you now?

CHARMAINE.   Right – out come the canisters. Smuggled off, out to South America – biggest market, right? And they love it, the big farmers. *Takes Dr. Skellman's watering can as if it were full of* D22. Full strength. *She waters.* Kills every bug in the bog, crops grow a treat, big money, get rich quick. Never mind the old peasants – poisoned for just handling the stuff. Never mind their kids out in the fields . . .

DR. SKELLMAN.   Hold on! You're well over the top! There's probably a very simple explanation.

CHARMAINE.   Why kill bugs over three years when you can do it in one? That's killer stuff.

Dr. Skellman puts her milk shake on a garden table.

DR. SKELLMAN.   Certainly. Undiluted it's lethal. But, come on, how do we know the government haven't called in ten more cans for testing? Something innocent like that?

CHARMAINE.   *Picking up Dr. Skellman's drink to finish it.* Be on one of the discs if they have. Les, I've got to know, I've got to do something. You got your keys?

Meopham House, evening

This is the country home of Sir Richard Johnson-Marshall, owner of J.M. Chemicals (UK) Limited. The elegant house, which harsh daylight would show to be in need of repair, is reached by a slightly weedy gravel drive. Mr. Martouf's white Mercedes approaches and stops beneath an ex-Rochester City Council lamp post.

Meopham House – the hall, evening

Housekeeper opens door to Mr. Martouf. Dinner for three is laid at the oak table. The place settings are adequate, not showy. One of the six wine glasses, for example, is odd. The carpets are good, but sparse, the furniture old leather. Sir Richard Johnson-Marshall is at the head of the table. He is about forty-five, overweight, with thick black curly hair. He is dressed for dinner in a dinner jacket and grey flannels. At one side of the table his old mother picks at her food and sips at her watered wine throughout the scene, ignored and ignoring. At the other side sits Stephen West. Mr. Martouf is shown into the hall by the housekeeper. Sir Richard stands. Puts on a brave face. Stephen West looks a bit scared, coughs on his food.

SIR RICHARD.   Mr. Martouf!

MARTOUF.   I was passing, Sir Richard. I felt the need to call.

SIR RICHARD.   And me harbouring the illusion I was off the beaten track. But a pleasant surprise.

Sir Richard takes a clean glass from in front of his mother and pours some wine for Martouf.

MARTOUF.   *Declining the offer of a seat, patrolling the room.* Perhaps one shouldn't harbour any illusions, Sir Richard. A dangerous game, that.

Sir Richard forces a smile, sits and cuts vigorously into his meat.

MARTOUF.   For example, my government has paid dearly for a commodity, yet delivery has not been made. One shouldn't mistake what would happen if that delivery were never made.

WEST.   It was the coastguards. We'd have lost the lot. We'd have been traced. It was prudent to –

SIR RICHARD.   And two days, three? What's a couple of days? It'll go again, I promise. You have an Englishman's word on that, my friend.

MARTOUF.   Good. I like the English gentleman's word: it always has the sound of a full stomach behind it. A beautifully pronounced passing of wind.

Sir Richard enjoys the joke for Martouf. Martouf comes back to the table.

MARTOUF.   We need that chemical, Sir Richard. So I do hope you'll keep your gentleman's word – one would hate to see the consequences of your not doing so.

J.M. Chemicals – main gate, evening

This is a security gate. The premises are surrounded by a ten-foot chain-link fence topped with a strand of barbed wire. Charmaine and Lesley drive up in Charmaine's white Panda Bianca with the top off. It has its name – 'Fred' – painted smartly on the front door. The car comes to the gate and stops. Charmaine toots for the security guard to come out. We see the glow of his small television. She has to toot again. The security guard comes out to the gate with his keys. But he has to skip a bit because he's in his socks. He opens the gate and the car drives through.

Westcotts' living room, night

Lyn is tidying the room. Open on a close-up of Sally's French book and its gruesome jacket. Lyn picks it up and puts it on a shelf. The TV news is on but we don't pay any attention to it. Lyn puts her 'Egg Sales' ledger and a print-out calculator into a bureau. She picks up Sally's Walkman and puts it on the French book. She looks at the television, slumps again at the pictures she sees. Now we notice the news, a report from a correspondent in the Middle East, with pictures to match.

CORRESPONDENT: ... In the long-running conflict between these warring states it is the ordinary people who suffer, who pay the price of the claims and counter-claims on this strip of infertile land: who pay the price with their lives ...

Dave throws open the door. He is greasy from repairing the tractor. As he comes in, fade up the sound of Ben coughing upstairs.

DAVE.   Can't you hear him shouting for you? He's coughing his guts up?

Lyn hurries upstairs. Dave remains for a moment.

Ben's bedroom, night

Ben is on the bed, coughing, head going from side to side on his pillow. He sits up, clutching his stomach.

BEN.   Mum!

Dave hurries in and bends over him.

BEN.   I got a ... bad pain ...

Lyn rushes in.

LYN.   *She cradles his head.* He's running a fever.

BEN.   *Coughs.* It's down here. *Holds his stomach.*

LYN.   Where? Show me. *She lifts his shirt.* There? There?

BEN.   An' here! *He clutches his throat.* Ow! Everywhere.

LYN.   Call Dr. Perritt. No, Dave, call the ambulance.

Ben looks wide-eyed, but is then suddenly and violently sick.

LYN.   Quick!

DAVE.   All right! *He rushes out.*

LYN.   It's O.K., love. You'll feel better now. *Calls.* Sally! Sally! Bowl and flannel. Hurry up!

Ben lies back, exhausted.

Westcotts' living room, night

The television is still on. Dave is at the telephone on the bureau. The sound of Ben still coughing upstairs.

DAVE.   I said I want an ambulance – and an ambulance is what I want. Thank you. Westcotts' farm, Fleetham. Yeah, on the marshes ...

Ben's bedroom, night

Sally comes in carrying a bowl and a flannel. Lyn is still comforting Ben.

SALLY.   *Sees the sick.* Err!

LYN.   *Grabs the bowl and flannel.* Get something to clean it up.

Ben just stares at Sally as she runs. Dave comes in.

DAVE.   It's coming.

LYN.   They'll need to know your mother gave him cowslip.

DAVE.   So? Cowslip's not poison!

LYN.   *Holding Ben's forehead as she washes.* Well done, Ben.

Ben sees Duke's picture on the wall above his head. He feels guilty about what he might have done to him, and begins to cry.

DAVE.   Come on, none of that. You're a farmer's boy, eh?

A sudden pain hits Ben. He catches his breath and starts coughing.

LYN.   I'll get you a glass of water!

She leaves.

DAVE.   Come on, lie easy now. Till the ambulance comes.

Ben stares at him, too ill to react.

J.M. Chemicals – reception area, night

Charmaine and Lesley Skellman come in from the main entrance and switch lights on.

CHARMAINE.   *Whispering.* Straight through?

Dr. Skellman nods.

CHARMAINE.   What we whispering for?

DR. SKELLMAN.   I'm not.

CHARMAINE.   You walked like you were whispering.
They go on through.

The laboratory annexe, night

Charmaine pulls the dust cover off her computer and switches it on.

CHARMAINE.   Stock in, stock out.

Charmaine takes a disc from a filing cabinet and boots it in. She watches avidly as she enters the page she wants. Dr. Skellman watches somewhat indulgently. The display comes up and Charmaine reads it. Now Dr. Skellman leans forward.

CHARMAINE.   See? Nothing out since they clapped it in irons. Not government, not nothing.

She looks at Dr. Skellman who shows no reaction.

CHARMAINE.   You counted 'em. We're ten cans short.
Les . . .

DR. SKELLMAN.   There could still be some logical explanation.

CHARMAINE.   Yeah, like half-inching – and get-rich-quick!

South Hill Hospital – Casualty Ward cubicle area, night

Ben is on a high bed with a transparent mask on for breathing. He is pale with rimmed eyes and his lips are wealing. A male nurse is giving full-time attention to Ben, who is conscious. Dave and Lyn are standing watching the activity anxiously. Dr. Reid, almost a child, comes to the cubicle and checks Ben's chart. She doesn't feel pressed to speak until she has finished. Her smile at Ben is very brief and businesslike.

DR. REID.   *To Lyn.* You're his parents?

LYN.   That's right, doctor.

DR. REID.   Has he ever had an attack like this before?

LYN.   No, never. It's out of the blue.

DR. REID.   Has he eaten or drunk anything unusual?

LYN.   His grandmother gave him some cowslip tea for a cough.

DR. REID.   *Notes with disapproval.* Natural concoction . . . Anything else?

Dave shakes his head.

DR. REID.   He's not got hold of any bleach in a lemonade bottle, nothing like that?

DAVE.   No way! Not on my farm.

DR. REID.   No sheep dip solution? No concentrated fertilizers?

DAVE.   I said, no way!

DR. REID.   *Back to Ben.* What do you say? You've not eaten or drunk anything you shouldn't? No strange berries?

Ben shakes his head.

DR. REID.   Mystery, mystery!

A dyke, night

The moon picks out a clear, straight stretch of dyke bordered by tall plants. Duke attempts to cross the dyke at a narrow point, but his legs fail him and he crashes into the water. He pulls himself weakly into the thick reeds, disturbing some sleeping moorhens which fly noisily away.

South Hill Hospital – Casualty Ward, night

There are lines of chairs with several casualties waiting. Sally is sitting hunched and tense near Ben, who is asleep. Dave and Lyn are standing talking to Dr. Reid who is leaning tired against a wall.

LYN.   He's a very honest boy, doctor. I know when he's lying. If he says he hasn't eaten or drunk anything he shouldn't, then he hasn't.

Dr. Reid looks at her blandly, almost disbelievingly.

DR. REID.   But he did have some herbal mixture this afternoon?

LYN.   At his grandmother's. Only cowslip tea. That's not . . . is it?

DAVE.   Can't blame that. He was ill before, that's why she gave it him. *Almost defiantly.* Perked him up!

DR. REID.   *More disbelief.* Anything else about the day you can think of?

LYN.   He didn't eat any supper. Didn't want it, did he?

DAVE.   You said.

DR. REID.   *Comes off the wall.* Well, we'll keep him in overnight. Do a few more tests. All right? *Somewhat awkwardly, she goes. Dave and Lyn look at one another.*

DAVE.   It's best. Best place.

Sally is choked at this, however logical it may be.

SALLY.   *Leaning forward.* We'll find Duke for you . . .

'The News' office the next day

Adam Roberts is on the telephone, the ace reporter onto a source.

ADAM.   Sure. Well . . . Yeah, can use it, I reckon. Yeah, O.K. Give us that number again. *He writes a phone number down.* Cheers. I'll get back to you. No, will do.

Bill Podger comes in from corridor.

BILL.   Met that Embassy mole yesterday. Got something to follow up.

ADAM.   Good on you.

BILL.   No, good on you. Directory of British Industries. South of England. I want all the chemical firms, anyone with trade to the Middle East.

ADAM.   But I'm onto –

BILL.   Library. Big red book.

ADAM.   *Indicates the phone.* He's –

BILL.   Next to the Directory of British Journalists-Out-of Work!

Adam sighs and gets up slowly.

Westcotts' farm – the side/back of the house

Dave comes from the barn towards the kitchen door. He passes the empty kennel, looks inside, as everyone does who passes.

Westcotts' farm – the kitchen

Lyn has all the domestic bottles of cleaners and bleach out from the cupboard under the sink. Sally is checking a plastic container of pills and medicines on the kitchen table.

SALLY.   *Trying an eye-drop bottle top.* Stuck an' all. No-one's had these for years.

Dave comes in.

DAVE.   He's done nothing like this.

LYN.   Course he knows. We've drummed it in enough.
And they're all in their proper bottles. Bleach says
bleach . . . *She starts putting them back.*

DAVE.   Facer then. I don't know.

SALLY.   And what's happened to old Duke?

Alice's house – the room

*Alice is getting up from kneeling at a full-length shallow
chest on truckles, interrupted in putting away some
unironed washing. She pushes it in. Dave is in the
doorway.*

ALICE.   You didn't come to ask me about no dog. He's
not a homing pigeon, he'd never come right out here
without young Ben.

DAVE.   It's a chance . . .

ALICE.   What did you really come to say?

DAVE.   Well, thought you ought to know. Ben. He's in the
hospital.

ALICE.   Davey! What's he done. Not been in an accident?

DAVE.   No, it's all right. Just a precaution . . .

ALICE.   Precaution? Precaution against what?

DAVE.   That bit of a cough. He was sick last night.
Coughing . . . and . . . real sick.

ALICE.   Davey! *She looks across at her rows of herbs.*

DAVE.   No, course not. Swallowed something, though,
done him no good. Thought you'd want to know.

ALICE.   Poor old mister . . .

DAVE.   It'll go through. We'll have him out in a day or
so.

ALICE.   Best place in the hospital is out of it! But I'll come and see him. And I'll be having a walk out with Jem, see if we can't find his old dog for him.

DAVE.   Yeah. That's the medicine he needs!

South Hill Hospital – Casualty Ward

Ben is lying half propped up in bed. He has a breathing mask to hand, but it is looped up and not being used. Lyn comes in with a polystyrene beaker.

LYN.   Little sip of drink?

Ben nods. He doesn't look too bad but he does have stomach ache.

BEN.   A drop.

LYN.   That's it. *She helps him.* You still can't remember drinking anything?

Ben shakes his head, takes another sip. Dr. Reid walks briskly in.

DR. REID.   *To Lyn.* Ah! I was looking for you.

LYN.   I got him a drink.

DR. REID.   I'd like a word. *She walks off into Sister's office.*

Lyn pulls a face for Ben, as if she's in trouble.

LYN.   I'm in trouble now!

Ben watches her sadly. There isn't a smile in him.

South Hill Hospital – Sister's office

Dr. Reid is in there, sorting through Ben's notes on the desk. Lyn comes in.

DR. REID.   We don't know what it is. Not as yet. He's more rested . . .

LYN.   Oh, he's a king to when he came in last night. It'll pass through.

DR. REID.   But having a lot of help from the medicines. Keeping him in check. I'm going to move him to London, get some more specialised tests done.

LYN.   London?

DR. REID.   King Henry's. They've got the facilities there, and more of the know-how. Whatever substance your son swallowed, it's unknown to us. They'll know it.

LYN.   But ... My husband ...

DR. REID.   Tell your husband it's very necessary.

Lyn stares at her. Sees Ben in bed, looking very weak and ill.

END OF EPISODE TWO

EPISODE THREE

M2 Motorway – Junction 5

A Kent County Council ambulance joins the motorway from the slip road, passing a sign saying 'London'. There are no flashing lights or sirens, but the ambulance isn't hanging about.

The ambulance

Ben is lying on one of the stretchers. An oxygen mask is nearby but is not being used. Lyn and a Staff Nurse are sitting on the other stretcher, Lyn nearer to Ben and holding his hand. The Staff Nurse has Ben's notes.

BEN.   Why aren't we going home? I can take medicine at home.

LYN.   More tests, that's all. Make sure. They've got better equipment in London.

Ben looks out of the darkened window. We see the country flashing past, through dark glass. He doesn't agree with her.

M2 Motorway – Farthing Corner Services

Still heading for London, the ambulance overtakes Brit and Scot's Land Rover, which is filtering off into the services area.

Farthing Corner Services, pedestrian bridge

From the London side, we see Brit and Scot on the covered road bridge, casually entering the services shop.

Farthing Corner Services – the shop

The shop is crowded with Sunday trippers returning from the coast, children wanting sweets and novelties, adults buying after-sun and cans of drink. Brit and Scot are at the cassettes, twisting the racks.

SCOT.   Billy Connolly! There's a comedian!

BRIT.   Here's another.

Stephen West comes to look at the cassettes. He's carrying a Sunday paper – three sections and a magazine. He twists the racks.

WEST.   *Publicly.* Anything good here?

BRIT.   All down to what you're after, son. An' out of interest – we don't usually jump-to Sundays.

WEST.   This is urgent. The boat's got to go again soon, there's a lot of pressure on, everything's getting a bit heavy.

BRIT.   Yeah? *Looks at Scot.* We ain't so sure now, are we?

Scot shakes his head.

BRIT.   *Indicates the paper.* Seen the stretches they're dishing out for that sort of traffic? Lot of risk for what we been paid . . .

WEST.   You've been paid to get the stuff across . . .

SCOT.   At the risk o' getting done? Old Bill out there in wet suits! Don' talk stupid, man!

A motorist comes up and looks at the cassettes. The trio move to the toys.

WEST.   All the same, the stuff's still here, isn't it? My man paid for delivery.

SCOT.   Then your man's gonna have to pay again! *Picks*

up a policeman doll. We're starin' at a seven, we get ourselves caught.

WEST.   So, how much?

BRIT.   Twice. Double. We're taking big risks.

WEST.   Double? He won't like that.

SCOT.   Tell him I do a ton o' stuff I don't like.

WEST.   It'll have to be soon.

BRIT.   Up front. Cash in hand.

WEST.   O.K. Rochester. Tomorrow night.

Scot puts the police doll back, lays it flat, stands a Scots doll on its stomach. They go to the till.

WEST.   *To the cashier.* Just the paper.

Brit and Scot pass behind him, empty hands held high.

SCOT.   Nothin' to declare.

South Hill Hospital – visitors' car park

The car park is packed for Sunday visiting. Alice threads her way through the jostle, holds herself aside to let a man hurry past and suddenly realises it's Dave.

ALICE.   Davey!

Dave is taken by surprise.

ALICE.   Said I'd come. How is he, Davey? What's going on with him, then?

DAVE.   *Trying to be matter-of-fact.* They've taken him to London. Lyn's with him. I'm getting the car.

ALICE.   London?

DAVE.   It's serious.

ALICE.   No . . . But he's a strong boy. He'll be fine.

DAVE.   They don't know what it is . . .

ALICE.   They don't know everything. *She faces him.* But you promise me you won't let them muck him about. *She looks all round her, disapprovingly.* Bring him to me. Eh? If he don't pick up, get him out. I'll see to him. Me and the marshes.

DAVE.   I've got to get off. I'll see you, Mum.

ALICE.   Promise! Bring him to me.

DAVE.   Got to go. I'll keep you posted.

Dave hurries off through the car park, Alice watching him.

King Henry's Hospital for Children – main entrance

The ambulance has arrived. Ben, in a sitting position and wrapped in a red blanket, is being carried into the hospital by the ambulance men. Lyn and the Staff Nurse go with him, the Staff Nurse setting her cap straight. Ben looks up and around him at the close, towering buildings.

BEN.   *Angry.* What's all this? I don't want all this!

Top of the escarpment

This is where the School Bus stops. Sally and Tony are walking up the track, Tony pushing his bike with an arm round Sally. Tony is sucking a piece of grass. They come to the metalled road where Tony prepares to cycle off.

SALLY.   Thanks for looking.

TONY.   Shame we didn't get a result.

SALLY.   Anyhow . . . *She stares at him.*

TONY.   See you tomorrow?

SALLY.   I'll consider it.

They kiss as Dave's car drives up.

SALLY.   No! It's my Dad.

Tony clips his trousers, gets ready to ride off. The car comes up to them, Dave staring.

SALLY.   'Lo, Dad. Er ... *She gestures towards Tony, as if to introduce him.*

DAVE.   Get my note?

Sally looks blank.

DAVE.   Kitchen table!

Sally shakes her head.

DAVE.   It says they've taken Ben up to London. So get yourself to Jordans, ask Alf to see to things. And pull old Henry in. I'm going up. Don't know when we'll get back.

SALLY.   Yeah. Dad, this is ...

DAVE.   And if you're worried – he'll be all right. It's only a precaution.

Dave turns the car, goes to say something else before driving off, but in avoiding Tony's bike he crashes his gears and then drives off in a rush.

SALLY.   London!

TONY.   He'll be all right, Sal ...

But Sally's feelings are now totally confused: happiness, sadness, guilt. Crying, she turns and runs down the track watched all the way by Tony.

King Henry's Hospital – Walt Disney Ward

A fine summer evening when hospital seems very hot and stuffy. This is a busy ward with children in and around the beds. Parents are sitting by very sick children or playing board games, etc. At the end of the ward a television is on.

*Ben's bed has the curtains round. Barbara James, a
nurse, pulls the curtains open. Ben is propped up in new
pyjamas in bed, being straightened up by Lyn.*

BARBARA.   Come on! Few days in bed, Benjamin. *She goes
on pushing the curtains open.*

BEN.   No! I don't have to be here. *To Lyn.* This is
stupid! *He coughs.*

LYN.   Ben!

BARBARA.   That's a cough you got there, not a singing
voice.

BEN.   Yeah? You ain't heard me sing!

LYN.   He's upset about his dog.

BARBARA.   His dog? You got a dog?

LYN.   A collie. Sheepdog.

*A human barking noise from Lee. For the first time we see
the next bed. Lee is lying on it, a boy of about Ben's age.
He is in dressing gown, pyjamas and slippers. He is bald,
and smiling at his own wit. He wears a Millwall shirt and
is broad cockney.*

BARBARA.   An' you behave yourself, Lee. *To Ben.* You'll
have to tell me about this dog, eh?

Lee barks again. Barbara ignores him.

BARBARA.   Don't get time for dogs, doin' this. An'
straightening troublesome boys!

Lee barks again.

BARBARA.   Shush now! That's no sort of welcome.

Lyn and Ben look at Lee.

LYN.   Hello, Lee.

Lee nods very briefly.

BARBARA.   There. You'll be just fine with us. Now what's upset you about your dog?

King Henry's Hospital – main gate, evening

Dave's car leaves with Dave and Lyn in it.

Dave's car

The car is travelling along the Old Kent Road towards Kent, Dave driving, Lyn red-eyed next to him. Biting her lip, Lyn looks back over her shoulder in the direction they have come. She swings back round as Dave swerves to avoid a car that has cut him up because he's wandered. Dave blows his horn, gets two back in return. Lyn looks at Dave's tense face, stares her unhappiness at him.

'The News' office at Wapping

Adam Roberts comes in clutching a large red directory. A computer print-out (of firms' names and addresses) is folded into it. He puts the print-out onto Bill Podger's desk and comes round to his own desk to place the directory down. He takes his notebook out, finds a telephone number in it and taps out the number on his phone.

ADAM.   Mr. Kennedy? Walter Kennedy, the School Governor? Adam Roberts, 'The News'. Sorry I didn't get back to you yesterday. No, not a lack of interest, not at all. Got a few minutes? There's a couple of basic background things I need to know.

King Henry's Hospital – Walt Disney Ward

Ben is out of bed at a window of the ward, looking down at the road. Everyone else is eating lunch, up at tables or in bed, some being coaxed by their parents. Barbara and the other nurses are busy pouring squash, tea, etc, helping in the odd spoonful. Lee is on his bed, picking at something, feeling too nauseated to eat. He pushes his tray aside.

LEE.   Go on, Ee-aye, jump out.

Ben looks round to check who Lee is talking to. He turns to the window again.

LEE.   High i'n it? It's the height does it. Further up you go, the higher you get.

Barbara James comes over and wordlessly tries Lee with a spoonful of his soup.

LEE.   *Turns his head away like a baby.* Don't want that. I'm telling him.

BARBARA.   Come on. Too much talking, if you ask me.

LEE.   I'm telling him about proper things. Don't know all this down Kent, do they? All country, and flowers, and pigs' muck. Different place, i'n it, Ee-aye?

BARBARA.   *Persisting with the spoon.* And he doesn't answer to Ee-aye. Good boy.

LEE.   *Swallows, closes his eyes with nausea.* Ee-aye, i'n it? *Sings.* "Ee-aye-adio, the farmer wants a dog!"

Ben doesn't turn.

BARBARA.   And that's enough of that! Now eat up or I'll roast you. *She comes over to Ben.* Of course the farmer wants a dog. Working tool, eh, Benjamin? Treated right. Turn 'em loose on the street, some folks near me. Family pets! Disgrace! Cruelty to animals. People like that don't even feel guilty.

BEN.   Who says? You can't see in their heads.

BARBARA.   *Surprised to have hit some nerve.* Oh, you *can* talk, Benjamin!

BEN.   *With a look at Lee.* Just 'cos I'm country I'm not stupid.

BARBARA.   Who says you're stupid? I'm country, and just as bright as anyone round here, thank you very much. *She picks up* 'The News' *from another bed.* Here want to read this? You like cricket?

Ben shakes his head.

BARBARA.   Well, plenty else. Cartoons . . .

BEN.   *For Lee.* We can read the writing an' all, down the country!

Alice's house

A beautiful day, with the sound of birds and the scent of flowers. Jem is lying contented in his kennel. Alice is sitting in the sun on an old backless chair, feet and legs apart, hands on knees as she listens to Dave's news.

ALICE.   Poison? They've said poison?

DAVE.   They don't know – except his inside's in a real state. It's all they can come up with.

ALICE.   He doesn't know what he took?

DAVE.   He doesn't know what time of day it is. With that, and the dog . . .

ALICE.   Lyn's with him?

Dave nods.

ALICE.   She's right. Be with him. *She jumps to her feet and goes into the house.*

DAVE.   *Following.* Course they're going through all the motions, checking out the school; the science lab . . .

Alice's house – the room

Alice goes to the drawer of her big table. From it she pulls sheaves of papers, large and small, old and new, all written-on recipe-style in pencil or in ink. Dave comes over to her as she sorts them.

DAVE.   . . . And the meals people. We've been through our place with a tick comb.

Still Alice searches in her papers, saying nothing.

DAVE.   It's not as if he's the sort of kid who'd ever . . .

Alice has found a folded paper and opens it gingerly.

ALICE.   Got it! *Confidently.* Davey, listen, you bring him to me. I've got all that's needed here. I'll swear by this. You bring him here to me, boy, don't waste his time.

DAVE.   Please . . .

ALICE.   Well, give 'em a day or two; but no more, you hear? Bring him back where he belongs. *Waves the paper.* We'll see to him. We don't need their fancy factory drugs.

DAVE.   I've got to go. Pick up Sally.

ALICE.   We don't, Davey.

DAVE.   She's over at Jordans. They'll have had more than enough of her chatter by now.

ALICE.   *Defiantly holds up her paper at him.* Davey!

DAVE.   I'll see you. An' I'll keep in touch.

ALICE.   *Lowers the paper, defeated.* Give him my love, then.

Dave nods, and goes. Alice puts the rest of the papers back in the drawer but keeps the piece she has been holding and places it under an ornament on the mantelpiece.

Westcotts' farm – front

Dave's car drives up with Dave and Sally in it. They get out and head for the house, automatically looking in the kennel.

SALLY.   No! We looked everywhere for him.

Dave opens the door with his key.

SALLY.   Everywhere. Tony and me.

DAVE.   Get some supper on. I've got a day's work to do.

A street in London

A busy thoroughfare dominated by a row of shops. All the London exteriors should be busy, noisy and crowded, in contrast to the country scenes. Barbara James, off-duty, comes to the entrance to her flat, which is between two shops. She is carrying a plastic bag of shopping. Adam is waiting for her in the doorway.

ADAM.   Hi!

BARBARA.   Oh. Hi!

Barbara tries to open the door one-handed but can't. Adam doesn't help until she pointedly gives him her bag to hold. They go in.

Barbara's flat – kitchen

A small, functional kitchen: formica'd and spotless. On the walls are magazine pictures of Sunny Jamaica. Barbara is sizzling some stir-fry vegetables in a saucepan, listening to music from back home. Adam comes into the kitchen, looking very pleased with himself.

BARBARA.   You look like the cat that got the cream –

ADAM.   Perhaps I did.

BARBARA.   You brought a bottle, then?

ADAM.   Just me.

Barbara looks at him.

ADAM.   You wait! Front page for sure. Well, page five: but leaded heads and a big by-line. Adam Roberts.

BARBARA.   *Has to be back at her stir-fry.* Very pleasing.

ADAM.   I've really got on the inside of this School Governor, some big noise in his borough and he's blowing the lid on this Headmistress. Zap! Going to school won't be the same again, not when they've read my piece.

He helps himself to fruit juice from the fridge and goes into the living room. Frowning slightly, Barbara tips some tinned meatballs into a saucepan. Adam comes back, biting into a banana.

ADAM.   Yeah, I think this is going to do Adam Roberts no harm at all. They're talking about Brett Pasco for the pictures. Pasco! Story by Adam Roberts, pictures by Brett Pasco!

Barbara suddenly becomes bright – not too falsely, but making him realise she's there, too.

BARBARA.   I had a good day an' all. Got Kelly using her caliper like a leg instead of a crutch. Gave a bit of comfort to a new little boy with some poisoning problem, and got to know about this dog he's lost. Oh, yes, I had a good day. *She runs her fingers like a by-line.* Barbara James.

ADAM.   *Dropping his banana skin noisily into the pedal bin.* Yeah?

Road to the Old Customs Houses

Brit and Scot's Land Rover with the two of them in it drives towards the Old Customs Houses. It stops close to the buildings and the men, after a quick look round, go inside.

The Old Customs Houses – upstairs room

Brit comes in, just checking. He reacts when he sees the tarpaulin out of place and the canisters in disarray. He starts counting the canisters. Scot comes in.

SCOT.   All O.K. below.

BRIT.   Well, it ain't up here.

SCOT.   *Surveying the scene.* Some old tramp, eh?

BRIT.   More like thieving kids! We're one short.

SCOT.   Well, plenty where they came from.

Brit gives him a look, jerks the tarpaulin.

BRIT.   Come on! An' nail up that door.

J.M. Chemicals – West's office

Stephen West is taking a telephone call.

WEST.   Just one? You're sure? Who – ? *He listens and appears reassured about the likely thieves.* Right. You'd better! And I'll see about one more.

J.M. Chemicals – warehouse

West is in the cage where the cans of D22 are stacked. He has a file with him and looks officially and innocently engaged, counting, checking seals on the cans, ensuring there is no leakage. As he comes out of the cage, firmly shutting the electronic lock, Charmaine crosses the warehouse from the loading bay. She, too, is carrying a file, about her business. We see her notice West.

CHARMAINE.   *Very 'innocently'.* All there, Stephen? Everything in order?

WEST.   I should hope so. Lethal stuff in the wrong hands.

CHARMAINE.   I forget what it was now.

WEST.   *As if she's a bit stupid, then.* D22, isn't it?

CHARMAINE.   No, what've we got?

WEST.   *Looks at his file.* Five hundred. Fifty thousand litres.

CHARMAINE.   Kill a few bugs, then!

WEST.   Will do. Anyhow, it's all secure, Charmaine. Don't lie awake nights. Five hundred, on the nose.

Dr. Skellman's laboratory

Lesley Skellman is working at her bench, clearly still on D22. Charmaine enters at speed, shuts the door behind her.

CHARMAINE.   Westie! Termite! Know what he's just said?

Lesley, interrupted, isn't best pleased.

CHARMAINE.   In the cage, just come out, "five hundred on the nose." Counted 'em! Five hundred!

DR. SKELLMAN.   He was counting them?

CHARMAINE.   *Nods.* In the cage. Five hundred, he said. Is he stupid? Or what?

DR. SKELLMAN.   He isn't stupid.

CHARMAINE.   Then, what?

King Henry's Hospital – Walt Disney Ward

A very poorly-looking Ben is sitting up in bed, reluctantly leaning over a board game with Kelly – a girl of about nine in a caliper – and Barbara. In the next bed Lee is lying asleep. The game they are playing is 'Sorry'. Ben has just turned over a 'four' card.

BARBARA.   Unlucky, Benjamin. Go back four spaces.

Ben doesn't bother. Barbara does it for him.

KELLY.   *Turns a card.* Two. *She moves a piece.* Another go. Ha! I'm winning you, Ben. You got no chance now.

BARBARA.   Don't you be so sure, Kelly Tate. It's a tight finish to this game, I tell you. *Turn a card.* Eleven. Can't use it. Benjamin?

Ben turns a card.

BARBARA.   Sorry! See?

BEN.   What I've always wanted! *With a weak finger he knocks in the nearest of Kelly's men.*

KELLY AND BARBARA.   Say it!

BEN.   *With bad grace.* Sorry.

BARBARA.   Now who's going to win? Different already, see? *To Ben.* Eh?

BEN.   Who wants to win anyway? Who wants to play stupid games?

Dr. Skellman's laboratory

Stephen West is standing over Dr. Skellman, at her bench.

WEST.   Sorry isn't always good enough, Lesley. Sir Richard wants to know when he can start getting his investment back.

DR. SKELLMAN.   Stephen – I hate to say this, but he wouldn't have an investment if I hadn't worked on it. And he certainly won't get it back until I've made it safe. It's lethal like it is.

WEST.   That's the idea, isn't it?

DR. SKELLMAN.   At the moment it's more like a chemical weapon. When I've made it safe and the government lifts its ban, Sir Richard can go laughing all the way to the bank.

WEST.   I'll tell him that. Meanwhile, he wants something for the government inspector when he comes next week. Some sign of progress.

DR. SKELLMAN.   Will they send someone who can count, do you think? Because there aren't five hundred cans still out there, Stephen.

West looks at her. What does she really know?

WEST.   No. Because our figures include the cans we're using for reseach.

DR. SKELLMAN.   Include? Do they?

WEST.   Oh, yes, It's only five hundred on paper.

Now Dr. Skellman knows he's lying.

King Henry's Hospital – Walt Disney Ward

Lyn and Barbara are talking in the ward doorway.

LYN.   He's worse, Barbara. Why can't they operate? Is it money? Or what?

BARBARA.   There's too many organs affected. It's the right antidote, that's what we want. The right reason.

Ben comes back from the lavatory carrying a papier mâché bottle of urine. His eyes never leave the floor.

BARBARA.   *To Lyn.* Excuse me.

Lyn realises she is being sent away. She goes. Barbara puts her hand out to take Ben's bottle.

BARBARA.   Thanks very much. Just what I wanted for Christmas, Benjamin. Keep drinking the water.

Barbara writes Ben's name on the bottle and stands it in a rack. Ben is about to slope off back to his bed, head down and deeply depressed.

BARBARA.   Hey! I want a word with you. Come over here. Come on.

Barbara takes Ben aside.

BARBARA.   Sit down there.

Ben sits on a low chair.

BARBARA.   So where you hurting? Eh? Where you hurting, Benjamin?

Ben shrugs.

BARBARA.   Stomach? Head? Back? Front? Sharp pain, dull aches?

Ben indicates his stomach. Barbara raises her eyebrows.

BEN.   Here. Dull.

BARBARA.   But we're giving you drugs to control that pain. You seem like you hurt other places, too. Only I want to know so I can understand you.

Ben shakes his head unconvincingly and slowly.

BARBARA.   Wouldn't be some pain outside?

Ben frowns, doesn't understand.

BARBARA.   Like some dog.

Ben stares at her: she's getting close.

BARBARA.   Did I tell you I had a dog once? Mister Dan, back home. Oh, he was some dog. Clever as yours, I'll bet.

BEN.   He'd have to get up early.

BARBARA.   Oh, yes. You want to know how he ended up? It was really bad. With his foot in a trap, somewhere I didn't know he was. And me, I never looked far enough, shrugged my shoulders and told myself he'd gone, and –

BEN.   You got stories like this for everyone? Cripple
stories for Kelly? Little cousins with leukaemia for Lee?

BARBARA.   Oh! There's something poison in there,
Benjamin, and it looks like a real bad dose of guilt
to me.

BEN.   You don't know!

BARBARA.   Don't I? Are you special or something,
Benjamin? Letting yourself slip away because your
dog's gone? Aren't you a country boy? Don't you know
about animals and the end of things with them?

BEN.   It's not the same as that.

BARBARA.   Oh no?

BEN.   *Finally.* You never killed your Mister Dan. Not
how I killed Duke.

BARBARA.   I never looked far enough. I could've found
him.

BEN.   Not like me. *He looks at her.* I drowned Duke.
How about that?

Barbara's expression doesn't alter.

BEN.   *A long pause.* It was hot, an' I took him in the inlet
with me.

BARBARA.   What inlet?

BEN.   There's this big place near us.

BARBARA.   You went in swimming? But they can swim
good, dogs. They can swim natural . . .

BEN.   We're not supposed to go in it. There's weeds, and
strong currents. But we did. Had a splash about, then
Dad came along looking for me, so I went under and
pulled Duke under till . . . Only Duke wouldn't have it,
I had to keep pulling him down, and he was fighting

me. And when I couldn't hold my breath no longer I
came up, and looked, and he'd gone, I'd lost him. He
wasn't there.

*Ben is just about fighting the tears. Barbara stares at him,
holds it.*

BARBARA.   Then let me tell you something, Benjamin.
You never drowned your Duke. Did you drown in all
that time you stayed under? Then he didn't neither. He
might have had a mouthful, but not enough to kill him.
He'd come up and cough that out.

BEN.   So where's he gone? How come he disappeared?

BARBARA.   Did you take a mouthful an' all, Benjamin?

Ben nods.

BARBARA.   Make you cough? Taste funny?

BEN.   Yeah . . .

BARBARA.   Listen – you didn't drown your dog, you get
that clear. Doesn't work like that, you get that right out
of your head. You start thinking to get yourself better,
an' no guilty conscience. Come on, treat yourself to a
drink.

*Ben isn't convinced as she walks him back across to the
main part of the ward.*

The marshes near to the sea wall

*Sally and Tony are out looking for Duke, one on each side
of a dyke leading towards the sea wall. This is where Alice
and Ben had been collecting plants on the first afternoon.
Sally and Tony are both in their after-school clothes as in
Episode One.*

SALLY.   *Puts out her hand to be helped across – keeps hold
of it.* What I feel really wicked about . . . I feel so

good. You know, Ben all ill, and Mum and Dad sick to death. And me, I'm thinking about something else all the time.

TONY.   You don't make your thoughts, do you? They just come. It's like saying a cat's wicked for going after a bird. You think about Ben, too.

SALLY.   Oh, yeah.

TONY.   And you're trying to help him, want to find out about his dog . . .

SALLY.   Yeah.

TONY.   Don't see what else you can do, then. *He kisses her quickly*. Anyhow, you'll soon get paid out if you're wicked.

SALLY.   Reckon? *She jumps back across the dyke*.

TONY.   Definitely. Come here.

SALLY.   Nope.

He jumps after her, misses his footing and falls flat in the dyke. Sally shrieks with laughter, pulls him out.

SALLY.   Who's been paid out? Tony Long, what have you been up to?

TONY.   *Down at his clothes*. Look at me!

She walks on towards the river. Suddenly she bends to the dyke side.

SALLY.   Here, Tony. Look!

Tony, dripping comes over and peers at the mud.

SALLY.   Could be . . .

We see what they see: a confusion of paw prints in the mud.

TONY.   Could be anything.

SALLY.   *Giving up, having come to the end of the dyke.* But we tried, eh?

She jumps the dyke to his side.

SALLY.   See? That's how we do it without falling in.

TONY.   Very skilled.

Tony bends to the dyke, gets a cupped hand of clear water, comes towards her.

SALLY.   *Running away.* Tony don't you dare.

She runs and he chases, up the concrete sea wall and onto the top. Where he splashes her with the water and runs himself, her chasing him now.

SALLY.   Tony! Tony Long! I'll tell my dad! I'll murder you when I get you!

The sea wall and the foreshore

The tide is going out revealing a stretch of uncovered mud. Sally catches Tony.

SALLY.   Right! You're going . . . in the mud.

TONY.   *Fighting her.* Oh no I'm not.

SALLY.   Oh yes you are!

Sally is about to give him a push down the sloping wall when she sees something in the river. She screams and it's for real.

TONY.   *Seeing it too.* Sal!

Now we see what they see. It is a dog floating by on the tide.

SALLY.   Duke! It's Duke! I know it is! Look!

Tony cuddles her. Sally breaks free and runs into the water but Tony catches up with her, holds her arm.

TONY.   Don't be stupid!

SALLY.   Let go! I'm going to get him!

But Tony doesn't let go. Sally stops pulling and they watch together while the dog floats on past.

END OF EPISODE THREE

EPISODE FOUR

The inlet

A different place to where Ben swam and where the canister fell in. Dave and a young male analyst are on the bank.

ANALYST.   *To Dave.* About here?

DAVE.   I told you I don't know; didn't see him. It's where we went in as kids.

ANALYST.   *Tests the water.* It's salt.

DAVE.   Would be, wouldn't it? Let's out into the river.

ANALYST.   Bit needle in a haystack. It's that dog you really wanted.

Dave nods.

Littlechurch Secondary School – classroom

The classroom is empty except for Sally, Jo and Lisa, who are at the back of the room. We can hear the sounds of pupils out at break.

SALLY.   It was horrible. He just went floating by ...

LISA.   In the river?

SALLY.   Course in the river.

JO.   Thought your Tony had dropped you when I see your face.

SALLY.   Not talking about him.

Jo and Lisa exchange looks.

JO.   So he's washed out to sea ... *She imagines what
happens next and pulls a face.*

LISA.   Who'd do something like that?

SALLY.   Ben's gonna cry his eyes out.

JO.   Best if he thinks the dog was just ill. Eh, Sal?
Better'n looking at everyone, and thinking all the time,
who done that?

LISA.   And it wouldn't be telling a lie. Not if they reckon
it's poisoned where he was swimming. Could be,
couldn't it?

JO.   Yeah, an' poison kills ...

*The significance of Jo's remark sinks in and the girls look
at each other. Sally sees the significance.*

King Henry's Hospital – Walt Disney Ward

*Ben is on his bed, taking a tablet watched by Barbara at
the drugs trolley.*

BARBARA.   That's it. Down the hatch!

*Lee is sitting on the side of his bed feeling a bit better,
flicking loose jigsaw pieces off his cover onto the floor.
Barbara moves on. Ben lies there with his eyes closed. He
isn't very well today. Lee comes across.*

LEE.   We go swimming down Rotherhithe Baths. Proper
water in there.

BEN.   We've got proper swimming pools.

LEE.   Oh, pools.

BEN.   Yeah, pools.

LEE.   Hot showers, we got. Caff. Machines.

BEN.   We got them.

LEE.   Don't get poisoned.

Ben looks at him.

LEE.   Then you 'ave to come up here to us to get you better.

BEN.   *Looks round, out of the window, pulls a face.* Rotten place. Noise and stink, like living down a drain. Turns you over just looking out the window.

LEE.   S'where I live, out that winder.

BEN.   Hard luck, then!

LEE.   Good luck! Proper people round 'ere, mate! Meat! Got no guts you country kids. Load of poncy 'orse ridin' an' lick my 'and, doggie. *Bored with this he turns his back on Ben.* Oi, Kelly – you got 'The Sun'?

'The News' office at Wapping

Adam Roberts is bending over his keyboard typing in a story, clearly enjoying the content of his piece. Opposite him, Bill Podger is taking a phone call. He puts down his phone and stares at Adam, not seeing him at first. He focuses on Adam, and Adam looks up.

ADAM.   I like to give 'em something gritty.

BILL.   Gritty? Is that the future tense of grotty?

ADAM.   Wait till you read this.

BILL.   *Coming round.* Not the School Governor and the Headmistress?

ADAM.   What else? Journalist of the Year for this.

BILL.   No – Wally of the Week.

Adam reacts.

BILL.   Haven't they said? It's dead, they won't print it. She can have us for libel from here to Timbuctoo, that Headmistress. Thought you'd been told.

ADAM. You're joking! It's a fantastic story.

BILL. Fantastic. But we can't print it.

ADAM. No way! I'm taking this to —

BILL. *Pushing a button on Adam's keyboard.* You're taking it out. Think of something else to make your name with. Think slush instead of grit. Oh, and watch out for a call from our Embassy friend. He's got hold of a sample of what they're dropping out there. We want it analysed and matched with anything British.

ADAM. That's leg work.

BILL. That's newspaper work. Even for this one.

Martouf's Mercedes

The car is being slowly chauffeur-driven on a sea front ride. It has come to a part of the front where the boating goes on. Martouf is next to the chauffeur, Johnson-Marshall and his mother are in the back. The window is down, and she is enjoying the sunny breeze on her face.

MARTOUF. The yachting scene! Messing about in boats. I get less jealous than seeing them at play on the beach, waiting for the tide to give them back their sand, all in the order of things, God in his heaven. No fighting for it, no bloodshed to reclaim the sand that's yours.

JOHNSON-MARSHALL. You've never been to Margate . . .?

MARTOUF. *Laughs.* The English wit! James Bond laughing in the face of death. Very heroic, and very unreal, when the real world's in turmoil, fighting its wars. *Suddenly direct.* We need what we've paid for very quickly now.

JOHNSON-MARSHALL. My dear fellow, it's hidden away, ready. We're making arrangements to get it to you.

MARTOUF. You said the same thing four days ago. I want action, enough of words. Even gentlemen's words.

Martouf turns and smiles at Lady Johnson-Marshall, who smiles back. The car stops. A hot dog seller is nearby. He sees Lady Johnson-Marshall, who nods like a child. He makes her a hot dog.

MARTOUF.   And I need more, much more. You do know that?

JOHNSON-MARSHALL.   More? Is that what this is about? Martouf, it can't be done – not the way it was before they locked it up. And separating molecules takes time.

MARTOUF.   That's what you're waiting for?

JOHNSON-MARSHALL.   *Nods.* Get a couple of cans past the inspectors and you shall have enough to take the world, I promise you . . .

MARTOUF.   I can't wait that long. Just get me thirty more. Fool your government, I don't care, but you get it out, you hear, Sir Richard?

JOHNSON-MARSHALL.   But what if I can't?

Martouf presses the electric button to raise Lady Johnson-Marshall's window, just as her hot dog is being handed in. Window cuts off the hot dog as car pulls away.

MARTOUF.   Then I dread to think what will happen.

J.M. Chemicals – Johnson-Marshall's office

Johnson-Marshall, a worried man, is standing at his desk, having had a bad and bloody shave that morning. West is sitting hunched at the back of the room. Dr. Skellman, also standing, has a file of test results with her.

JOHNSON-MARSHALL.   So how long do I have to wait to get my product safe to ship? I've got a million pounds of marketable stock out there, Lesley.

DR. SKELLMAN.   *Opening her file.* I think I've found the answer, Sir Richard.

JOHNSON-MARSHALL.   Ah!

DR. SKELLMAN.   *Closing her file again.* The answer is –
there isn't an answer. There is no magic solution. Some
molecules won't separate the way we want them to. I've
tried every formula, and ... I'm sorry but there's
nothing to do except dilute it.

WEST.   What?

DR. SKELLMAN.   We'll just have to reduce our profits,
dilute and pay more for transportation. It'll still do the
same good ...

JOHNSON-MARSHALL.   You are sure? You are very sure?

DR. SKELLMAN.   Certain.

There is a long silence, finally Johnson-Marshall sits.

JOHNSON-MARSHALL.   *To Dr. Skellman.* Oh, go.

DR. SKELLMAN.   *She goes.* I'm very sorry.

JOHNSON-MARSHALL.   Why did I know she was going to
say that?

WEST.   There is another way.

JOHNSON-MARSHALL.   That leaves me alive?

WEST.   I've got access to the sealed area for safety checks.

JOHNSON-MARSHALL.   Oh, we can get in and out. It's
those blasted cans stuck there.

WEST.   Then we substitute. Put something else in,
something look-alike, and take out what we want.

JOHNSON-MARSHALL.   We?

WEST.   It can be arranged.

King Henry's Hospital – Walt Disney Ward

*Mr. Murray-Mott is at Ben's bed, with Sister O'Hara
and Barbara.*

MURRAY-MOTT.   *To Sister O'Hara.* You say the water sample was negative? Nothing from this inlet?

SISTER O'HARA.   It's tidal, like testing the River Thames itself.

MURRAY-MOTT.   *To Ben.* And you drank nothing naughty? No sipping your father's chemicals to grow hairs on your chest?

BEN.   No.

MURRAY-MOTT.   And when you went for your little swim – did it have a funny sort of taste, eh, like nasty medicine?

Ben shakes his head.

MURRAY-MOTT.   Mmmm. You know they call us the Flying Squad round here? Well, we pretty generally get our man. You're the scene of the crime, and we're here to nail the culprit, eh? Now I'm going off with all the evidence.

Ben stares at him, unimpressed. He has hated all this close, crowded-in attention, and it shows. Mr. Murray-Mott and Sister O'Hara go on to the next bed.

BARBARA.   All right, Benjamin? Can't say you're lacking for attention.

BEN.   I've had it with all this! *He shows the claustrophobia with raised hands.*

BARBARA.   I know what you mean. Here, I brought this to show you. *She takes a small photo album from her pocket which she opens.* See? Our little house in Savanna-la-Mar, Jamaica. And my mam. And my brother the day he got married – looking like the king of all the world and terrible nervous all at once. And views, Benjamin, what I look out on. Very pleasing, eh? And August the second, I'm going to be there.

BEN.   How much to come with you?

The phone rings in the ward office. Sister O'Hara passes to answer it.

BARBARA.   How much you got? You get your mam to bring in one of these for you. Makes these walls like windows, just for the odd five minutes.

'The News' office

Adam is on the phone, leaning back. Bill is typing a story in, just the quiet click of computer keys.

ADAM.   Which Sister is this? Ah, Sister O'Hara. Sorry to trouble you again. Social Services, Duty Officer here, Area Three. You've got a patient in from Kent, young boy been poisoned? We're just checking on the family, North Kent, haven't given us all the details: they're not on the case file, anyhow. Now, what's the boy's name? *He makes notes.* And his date of birth? O.K. And can you confirm the home address for us? Yeah, that rings bells. How's he doing, by the way? *He writes this quote down, a sad face on.* Yeah, Duke! Yes, well, thanks a lot for your help.

Adam puts down the phone and starts tapping his story into the computer.

King Henry's Hospital – Walt Disney Ward – recreation room

Barbara is sitting in an armchair working at some files. Children are engaged in quiet activities like drawing, reading, doing puzzles. There is no television. Children's paintings are on the walls. Kelly is reading, Lee is felt-tipping a violent picture, and making bombing noises, Ben is writing in an exercise book which he has illustrated with various breeds of sheep dog. Kelly frowns at her book. She looks round for Barbara but she's too busy. She tries to read on, but the book makes no sense. Lee is nearest to her. She limps across to him.

KELLY.   Lee – what's this?

LEE.   *Still at his picture.* Dunno.

KELLY.   This word. I don't know what a . . . this is.

LEE.   What a what is? Gi's it. *He snatches the book.* East-Enders!

KELLY.   Grange Hill.

LEE.   Where?

Kelly points.

LEE.   *Quickly, handing back the book.* Lavatory.

KELLY.   Lavatory?

LEE.   Lavatory. Toilet. Bog. *He opens his mouth again to go on.*

KELLY.   *She reads her page again.* Still don't make sense.

Lee ignores her, makes more loud bombing noises.

LEE.   Bombs away!

BARBARA.   Lee! Less of the noise!

Kelly flaps her book down. Ben looks over.

BEN.   Wassup? Where?

KELLY.   'Mrs. McLusky'. That bit.

BEN.   *Reads.* 'Mrs. McLusky had come to a decision. She had to close the laboratory. That or run the risk of someone making stink bombs again.' Yeah?

KELLY.   Laboratory . . .

BEN.   Where they do science.

KELLY.   *To Lee.* It weren't lavatory, it was laboratory. All about stink bombs.

LEE.   Makes me right then, don't it?

KELLY.   Ben's a better reader than you. You're stupid.

LEE.   *Throws down his felt tips.* Yeah? I'll read you a story. Gi's this. *He takes her book. As if reading from the book.* Once upon a time there was this nobby pillock from down the country an' Ee-aye was his name. Worse than a little baby, he was, about being up London 'stead of down the country. Didn't like it up London 'cos the buildings was too high. Didn't like the noise 'cos no-one could hear him cryin' for his mum. Didn't like the walls all round 'im 'cos they was made of bricks instead of cows' muck.

Ben turns his back on Lee, tries to get on with his work.

LEE.   One day – you lis'ning Ee-aye? – he had this dog and this dog barked at him, woof-woof, and Ee-aye was so scared he bottled it and ran away and ran and ran and ran and ran, and the dog never ever found him again.

BEN.   Shut up!

LEE.   You gonna?

BARBARA.   Here! Half-time, you two!

KELLY.   Lee's telling a good story.

LEE.   So he didn't shut no-one up, he bottled like the Chelsea, an' the nurse come to his rescue.

BARBARA.   An' that's enough of that!

Ben sizes Lee up, then turns his back again.

KELLY.   *To Lee.* Go on! What happened to the dog?

LEE.   Ask him. He'll tell you. *He throws the book at Ben's head.*

A London bus

Lyn is sitting next to a man reading 'The News'. *She has grapes, a few trade magazines and a bottle of squash. The bus stops. Several passengers get out. The man next to Lyn goes, leaving his copy of* 'The News' *on the seat. Idly, Lyn picks it up, flicks through it without really seeing. Suddenly she turns back a page and focuses on a story. She is disbelieving, then shocked, finally angry. She throws the paper down, picks it up again and reads it once more. We see the headline of the story she is reading:* 'Swimming Boy in Poison Horror.'

King Henry's Hospital – Walt Disney Ward – ward office

Sister O'Hara is standing behind a chair facing a very angry Lyn.

LYN.   *Thrusting* 'The News' *at her.* 'Swimming Boy in Poison Horror'! Lovely, isn't it? 'What's in the water at Fleetham?' See that? 'A young Kentish lad wants to know because he's dying from it'! Dying?

SISTER O'HARA.   Let me see it, then.

LYN.   Yes, you see it! What the hell's going on? Why don't you put it on the news? John Craven? And who says he's dying? No-one's said that to me.

SISTER O'HARA.   They've made that up, Mrs. Westcott.

LYN.   Who? How? Who made it up?

SISTER O'HARA.   *Waves the paper.* These people. They said they were Social Services. They telephoned.

LYN.   Telephoned? And you told them? Were you born yesterday?

SISTER O'HARA.   *Rallying.* I was not.

Lyn looks out of the office window to where Ben is lying hunched away from everyone, in bed.

LYN.   If he sees this paper you'll wish you'd never been!

A pub near London Bridge

Adam, with a friend from 'The News' office, is in a booth, imitating the Fleet Street tradition. Adam is on white wine, the other on a fashionable beer. They are laughing like schoolboys. Barbara comes in with a copy of 'The News'. She comes straight to Adam, throws it on his table, knocking over his wine glass.

BARBARA.   You trash! You connivin' little rat!

ADAM.   *Suddenly cold.* And I didn't know you loved me!

BARBARA.   You eat my food, you drink my drink, an' you take stuff I say to you an' shove it in your filthy gutter rag – all for the glory of your trashy name in the paper. You nearly got O'Hara suspended, you know that? But you don't care! You don't mind what you do 'long as it's O.K. for Adam Roberts! Well, I think you stink to high heaven! Just you be sure your face don't come round my corner any more! You hear?

ADAM.   Wait a minute. You never said ...

BARBARA.   Never said? I said too much!

Barbara is in the mood to do more damage with the beers – but she doesn't, and she goes, slamming the door. Adam shrugs to his friend.

ADAM.   Sorry about that. One of my fans.

Annexe to Dr. Skellman's laboratory

Charmaine is sitting in her chair, swivelled away from her computer. She is tucking into an individual pork pie, reading 'The News', *eyes on stalks, shocked. Lesley Skellman comes from her laboratory.*

DR. SKELLMAN.   Reading your stars? Don't fancy your luck if you are!

CHARMAINE.   *Thrusts the open paper at Lesley.* Kid swimming in the inlet! Dying! Lesley, that's round here. What price those missing cans now?

Lesley Skellman reads the article.

CHARMAINE.   And what price that little creep West? I tell you —

DR. SKELLMAN.   *Very sharply.* No don't Charmaine! Just for once.

Charmaine is shocked at this reproach from Lesley.

DR. SKELLMAN.   *Quietly.* I made that stuff, remember?

King Henry's Hospital – Walt Disney Ward

Ben is sitting up on his bed, dressed and in slippers, but otherwise looking very ill. Lyn is with him. Alice is coming in, escorted by Dave and Sally.

BEN.   Nan!

ALICE.   Threatened you I'd come, didn't I?

Dave and Lyn exchange looks – they'll talk about the newspaper piece and the hospital later. Alice kisses Ben on the forehead with ceremony, like a blessing.

SALLY.   'Lo, Ben.

BEN.   Wotcha.

ALICE.   *Taken aback at how bad he looks.* How are you then, mister? How you feeling inside?

Ben shakes his head: not well. Alice moves away from the chair which Dave has put for her, offers it to Lyn.

LYN.   I'm all right, Mum. Sit down.

SALLY.   *Gives Ben a small photo album.* Here, what you wanted.

LYN.   And look after them, they're precious.

Ben wants to open it, but with Alice his special visitor he doesn't. Lyn and Sally sit on the bed, Dave on a chair with his back to Lee, who is lying on his own bed. Alice sits.

ALICE.   Here, mister, see what I've brought you. *From her straw bag she produces a sewn packet of herbs. Lee sits up and takes an interest.*

BEN.   Thanks, Nan.

ALICE.   Put that under your pillow and you'll go to sleep smelling the hedgerows.

Lee blows a slow, reflective raspberry. Dave turns and looks at him, and Lee stares back.

ALICE.   Down along Rye Common I went for those, and along Hope Fleet. You won't know you're not back there, in your dreams.

Lee makes a snoring noise, which everyone ignores.

BEN.   Ta. *He puts the sachet under his pillow, quickly.*

LEE.   *To Kelly.* Any papers?

KELLY.   Dunno. They've hid 'em all.

LEE.   Dilks! Wasson telly? *He goes off down the ward.*

Dave looks at Lyn: some relief.

LYN.   *Opens Ben's album – at Duke.* Come on. Touch of home, eh?

BEN.   Was. You seen nothing of him?

ALICE.   No, mister, tide won't bring him back, it don't work like that, do it?

SALLY.   *Hushing her.* Nan!

Ben looks puzzled.

ALICE.   Eh? Well, it's foolish living on hope. Out to sea is out to sea. It don't do to think otherwise, not in my book.

BEN.   Out to sea?

No-one knows quite what to say.

ALICE.   Don't he know, then?

BEN.   Don't I know what?

ALICE.   *Taking a stand.* No. You should've told the boy, Davey.

LYN.   Shut her up, can't you.

DAVE.   Mum, you don't know everything yet.

ALICE.   Don't he know? Davey! You can't keep a kid hanging on the hope of something that's never going to happen. I'm not being a party to that. No, I'm not.

BEN.   *Shouting at them.* What? What don't I know?

DAVE.   Voice!

LYN.   No! Her! Tell her! Dave ..!

Others in the ward are looking round now.

ALICE.   *Standing her ground.* He was in the river. That's where he was, and that's where he's gone, on the tide. Taken away peaceful. I'm sorry, boy, I don't go along with your mother. I reckon you ought to know.

BEN.   Oh! Duke!

LYN.   Take her home, will you?

ALICE.   All right, Lyn. I don't need to be taken. Mister, he wasn't shot, wasn't trapped, he didn't suffer that way. That's something, eh?

She smiles at him. They all wait for his reaction.

BEN.   It was the water, Barbara said. He drank it, and now he's dead.

LYN.   That's only a theory. They have to have theories.

BEN.   He's dead. And now . . .

SALLY.   You're not going to die.

DAVE.   Load of rubbish. No proof at all.

ALICE.   Come on, now, mister, it's not the end of the road, not by a long chalk.

LYN.   Of course, it's not. And no thanks to you, you stupid old witch!

Top of the escarpment

Adam drives up in a small Fiat and parks. He gets out holding a map, checks where he is and throws the map back into the car, which he locks. He walks off down the track.

The inlet's edge

This is near the Old Customs Houses, where Ben went in swimming. Adam comes to the edge and surveys the water. He bends to it, dips his finger in and goes to taste it with the tip of his tongue, but he thinks better of it and wipes his finger on his trousers. He follows along the inlet's edge and comes to a little creek. Peering into the water he sees something, under the weeds. He goes into the bushes for a stick, comes back and fishes out the empty canister, dropped previously. He looks carefully at what remains of the taped seal. We see what he sees printed on it. 'J.M.

Chemicals.' *He strips off the seal and pockets it. Holding the can, he walks on round the bank, looking for more.*

J.M. Chemicals – reception area

A small area where customers and reps are seen, with farming and chemical magazines about. Adam is holding the canister, walking upstairs.

WEST.   *Tosses the newspaper back at Adam.* Very heart-rending – but there's nothing sinister about that can, believe me. *Thinks.* Have a look at it. Is there a number embossed there, underneath? A code of some sort?

ADAM.   *Looking.* And if there is?

WEST.   What is it?

ADAM.   What, the numbers? *Stops.* Can't you tell me?

WEST.   Adam, there are hundreds of combinations. I'm not playing some game.

Adam holds up the can. He is wearing his watch inside his wrist.

ADAM.   MC stroke seven three zero B.

Stephen West goes over to computer. We cannot see the screen.

WEST.   *Head down.* Zero stroke B?

ADAM.   *Reads his watch again, which we now see in close up: MC/730B.* MC stroke seven three zero B.

WEST.   Zero B . . . *He keys in another code.* Yes, thought so. One of a faulty batch. Normal thing is, we put it out for scrap; this chap must have fallen off the dust cart. *Shrugs.* Nothing more than that. We've got a very clean bill of health round here. And we never used that can, sir. End of the story, sorry.

ADAM.   Where's it faulty, then? Looks all right to me.

WEST.   In the seam's the usual place. Only a single weld? Which is all right for baking powder, but not for what we make.

ADAM.   Which is what?

WEST.   *Gives him a pamphlet.* Agricultural chemicals: insecticides, pesticides, that sort of thing. We kill the creepy-crawlies that eat up people's crops.

ADAM.   *A sudden thought.* Nothing for anyone's army?

WEST.   Definitely not! Strewth! Here, why don't you do a piece on the good we do? It's all in there.

ADAM.   Not news, is it? Well, cheers, anyway.

As Adam picks up his can ready to go, Charmaine comes through, crossly clearing the computer.

CHARMAINE.   *To West.* MC seventy-three zero B. Was that you mucking about?

ADAM.   Canister batch.

Charmaine looks surprised. Adam holds up the canister.

CHARMAINE.   Oh, canisters.

ADAM.   *To West.* Keep the paper.

West shows him to the door. Charmaine is curious at the paper. She looks at the page, open at the Ben story. She doesn't need to read it.

WEST.   *Calling after Adam.* Good to get it sorted. *He comes back.*

CHARMAINE.   *Nowhere near the paper now.* What did he want?

WEST.   Nothing for you to worry your purple head about.

Road by Westcotts' farm

Adam in his Fiat drives slowly past, giving the place a good once-over. Dave's car, returning from the hospital, arrives. Lyn and Sally are in it, Alice having been taken home. The two men eye each other and Adam drives off.

The White Swan

It is evening opening time, a few people are in the bar. The barmaid has served Adam with a Perrier, although his back is to us and we don't immediately see who he is. Lesley Skellman is at a table with an orange juice, waiting for Charmaine to return from paying. Lesley has 'The News' with her.

CHARMAINE.   . . . Anyhow, he had hold of one of our cans, been in the wet somewhere.

Lesley Skellman's eyes change focus to someone beyond Charmaine.

CHARMAINE.   You know! A canister, D22 – one of ours, what's missing! *She looks round to see Adam standing listening.* Oh, shut your mouth, Charmaine!

ADAM.   Missing? Not what your Stephen said. Scrap, he told me.

DR. SKELLMAN.   Sorry?

ADAM.   'The News'. That's my piece.

Lesley Skellman looks back at the paper.

ADAM.   All my own work. What's this D22, then? *Waves his pamphlet.* Doesn't rate a mention in here.

DR. SKELLMAN.   You found a canister in the water?

ADAM.   Got it in my car.

DR. SKELLMAN.   Empty?

ADAM.   Of what? D22?

DR. SKELLMAN.   *Indicates the paper.* Is this sort of thing supposed to help get him better?

Adam shrugs. Lesley Skellman sits and drinks her drink.

CHARMAINE.   *She comes back to Adam.* So you write this stuff? If you went in that phone box would you come out as Superman?

ADAM.   With the right phone card. Hasn't failed yet.

CHARMAINE.   If I wear a cape, it gets in the way.

ADAM.   Depends what you're doing.

CHARMAINE.   *A pause.* Swimming.

ADAM.   Round here?

CHARMAINE.   Not any more, bet your expenses on that.

DR. SKELLMAN.   You didn't say where this child was. Which hospital.

ADAM.   We like to protect our sources.

CHARMAINE.   How'd you like to protect your specs from a Coke in the phizog? Come on, where is he, Superman?

ADAM.   King Henry's. Walt Disney Ward. Benjamin someone. Mean anything?

DR. SKELLMAN.   You couldn't show us where you found the can, could you?

ADAM.   Could do. If you do something for me.

CHARMAINE.   Wheeler-dealer!

ADAM.   You've got a lab. Would you look at some stuff I'm getting from a contact?

DR. SKELLMAN.   Analyse it? What is it?

ADAM.   Dangerous.

Dr. Skellman's cottage – front room

Lesley Skellman is on the telephone. Charmaine is perching nearby with an apple.

DR. SKELLMAN.   There's nothing I can be certain about yet, but if you've done all the tests at King Henry's . . . I'm sure, yes. Well, I'm going to assume that it's D22 poisoning, and I'm going to start work on an antidote. Of course I'll keep in touch. *She puts the phone down.*

CHARMAINE.   Right. And I'm going to Sir Double-barrelled Double-barrelled about that can in the water. I bet West never told him. Nor about all the others.

DR. SKELLMAN.   I'll come with you.

CHARMAINE.   You don't have to hold my hand. Yes, you do: that man gives me the shivers.

King Henry's Hospital – Walt Disney Ward

A film is on the ward television watched avidly by those patients well enough to do so. Lee is among them. The ward is very crowded with people – patients, parents and staff. Ben is seated in an armchair, crowded in by people. It is very noisy. He has his photo album in his hands. He is looking at it but not really seeing. His face tells us that he is staring at the probability of his illness being fatal. Barbara crowds past him with a covered tray of treatment for someone down the ward. Her thigh knocks the album from his hands to the floor.

BARBARA.   Sorry, Benjamin.

Barbara goes on and Ben picks up the album. He opens it again. We see the photographs of himself and Duke taken from his bedroom wall. Ben lingers on an enlarged picture of Duke, then turns the page and there is a happy snap of himself and Alice, squinting in the sun. He turns another page to a wide, flat view of the marshland. This view, now cine, fills the screen. The ward noises fade to silence, and

*the muted sounds of sea birds, sheep, and a dog barking in
the far distance fade up. As the camera pans, the
soundtrack is gently overlaid with Ben's music. Ben's arm
suddenly comes across the picture and wipes it as he nurses
his stomach against a bad pain. Ben's theme runs into the
film-closing music, and the ward noises – the voices, the
clatter, the crying and a persistent bleep – swell as people
move from the television and jostle and crowd round him.
On his own way back from the television, Lee suddenly
snatches up Ben's album.*

LEE.   What you been 'iding, Ee-aye?

BEN.   Give us that!

LEE.   Ha! *He barks like a dog at the picture of Duke, turns
a page.* This you? Whoa! Who's this ol' woman? She
ain't the one started the all-off yesterday?

BEN.   *Gets up.* Give it here! I've bloody had it with you!

*Lee holds the album above his head. Ben grabs at it but
fails, and in the tussle Lee falls backwards onto the floor,
lying there surprised at his own weakness.*

BARBARA.   Benjamin!

King Henry's Hospital – main entrance

*A summer evening, but overcast. The streets are as busy as
ever, with queues of traffic and crowded pavements, people
to-ing and fro-ing around the hospital. Ben runs out of the
main entrance, a hand held tightly across the pain inside
him. He dodges among ambulances, cars and pedestrians as
he makes off up the street. As he pushes out through the
hospital doors, city music starts on the beat of their swing,
discordant and frantic.*

City streets, evening

*Ben is running with the hopeless aim of getting home. He
looks this way and that, heading off in the direction the*

ambulance brought him from. He is dressed in jeans and a jersey. People crowd around and above him. Cars, heavy lorries, taxis, buses all cut him close, with fumes, revving, impatient honking and angry shouts. The buildings tower above and seem to go up forever, joining the sky and allowing no light. His run, which is weakened by illness and slowed by pain, is accompanied by the discordant musical theme, insistent and frightening. Ben bumps into someone, who swears at him. The music builds to a climax as Ben gets more bewildered. He turns corners in his panic, hating this place, running, leaning for rest, running again – till at the climax of music and oppressive images he runs round a final corner and finds himself facing the hospital once more: back where he started, trapped in the city street. His face shows his loss of all hope – and a sudden surprise.

BARBARA.   Benjamin! *She emerges from the crowd to grab his arm.* Come on. Come with me, mister.

Ben looks at her, exhausted, but surprised at hearing Alice's form of address.

Meopham House – the library

One bar of an electric fire is burning in the large fireplace. In a winged armchair Johnson-Marshall's mother sits before a large jigsaw puzzle. The matching chair is empty, Johnson-Marshall standing behind it. The puzzle they are making is of grown-up fairies, Beardsley-style. Lesley Skellman and Charmaine are sitting knee-to-knee on a drawn up settee.

JOHNSON-MARSHALL.   A sick boy? On D22? Really, Lesley, I have to ask: what sort of rubbish is this?

DR. SKELLMAN.   I don't think it's rubbish, Sir Richard. Not necessarily.

JOHNSON-MARSHALL.   But it's all so much
fantasy . . .

CHARMAINE.   Fantasy? Ten cans of killer-diller missing
out of the cage? That's real. One empty can gets fished
out of the water? That's real an' all. A kid who goes
swimming there gets poisoned? How real does real have
to be? *Suddenly polite.* Sir Richard?

JOHNSON-MARSHALL.   Whether it's a seeming reality or
some sort of fantasy, it's still fiction, dear.

CHARMAINE.   *Seriously and quietly.* I think you've got a
duty to do something about it, anyhow. Look into it, or
something.

JOHNSON-MARSHALL.   *Sighs.* Will it make you happy,
Lesley?

DR. SKELLMAN.   Happier. Yes, much, Sir Richard.

Charmaine goes to open her mouth.

DR. SKELLMAN.   O.K., no-one knows for sure. Perhaps
we're putting two and two together and making five.

CHARMAINE.   But I've counted the cans.

*Johnson-Marshall comes round the chair, thinking.
Automatically, he guides his mother's hand to place a piece
she's been holding while she stares her dislike at the young
women.*

JOHNSON-MARSHALL.   You've not told anyone else about
your counting?

CHARMAINE.   Only –

DR. SKELLMAN.   Only me.

JOHNSON-MARSHALL.   I shall telephone the police. How's
that? A commissioner I know, tonight, without fail. And
thank you for informing me – for your loyalty to the
company.

This is the signal for Lesley Skellman and Charmaine to get up.

DR. SKELLMAN.   Goodnight, Lady Johnson-Marshall.

Meopham House – the hall

CHARMAINE.   Only I wouldn't mind betting this stuff could be used for all sorts. Killer-diller! Fanatics, lobbing it at other people, dropping it on 'em.

JOHNSON-MARSHALL.   *Stares at Charmaine.* Frightening. I'll phone tonight.

CHARMAINE.   Then we'll see the boys in blue tomorrow?

JOHNSON-MARSHALL.   Hopefully.

Awkwardly, Johnson-Marshall shows them out. We hear the front door shut.

Meopham House – the library

A very worried Johnson-Marshall returns. He shuts the door, stands inside it, thinking. Goes to the phone and picks it up with resolution.

JOHNSON-MARSHALL.   I never wanted anyone hurt.

Outside Meopham Hall

Dr. Skellman's car leaves.

END OF EPISODE FOUR

EPISODE FIVE

A Scrap Yard

This is Brit's and Scot's legitimate business – scrap. Their yard in Chatham is corrugated-fenced with a Portakabin office. Scot is talking to two rough-looking men. Brit is in the open-doored Portakabin office with sheaves of paper and bulldog grips. He handles them all roughly. A local radio station is playing pop on a dirty transistor. Stephen West drives into the yard, gets out of his car, dressed casually.

BRIT. *Out quickly. Drops his voice.* Told you not to show your face here. *Tries to steer West back to his car.*

WEST. If you don't answer your phone . . .

BRIT. Weekend! You don't own me, son.

Scot comes over.

SCOT. Come on, on your bike, you! *Looks round nervously.* You gone mad?

WEST. I've got to talk. It's urgent.

BRIT. 'Urry up, then. We get a lot of attention . . .

WEST. Date. We've got to be ready to go this week. No ifs and buts and the state of the tide – we've got a rendezvous with a ship.

BRIT. A ship?

WEST. In the river. And I've got twenty cans dressed up as chemicals, we've to get them into the plant one night and get the real stuff out.

SCOT. More in an' more out?

BRIT.   That's hard!

WEST.   It'll be easy enough. I'll sort that end of it when I've done here.

BRIT.   It'll cost you.

WEST.   In for a penny, in for a pound. And there's something else. What if my man wanted a couple of females off the scene for a while?

Brit whistles in his teeth.

SCOT.   Concrete job?

WEST.   *Shakes his head.* Just out of the way. Mystery disappearance. As if they've gone off on holiday.

BRIT.   Oh, you're talking very serious now, son. You'd better come in the office, give us a few details.

The East Kent Trials

A large field with marquees and side shows, not too grand. There are pony events, a young farmers' wellie-throwing contest, etc., all going on in a small arena. But the main attraction, over which people become very serious, are the sheep dog trials: the finals of which, senior and junior, are held in the large field. Enthusiastic youngsters are helping with the parking in a side field. We open with a general view of the activities: in particular, the off-loading from a lorry of a flock of sheep into a holding pen. Canned music is playing until the trialling begins, and the loudspeaker announcements are low key as yet, mainly organisational: "Would Mrs. Sherriff go to the women's institute tent?" "Mr. Garland, please let the judges know when you arrive."

The car park

Barbara's old mini turns into the field, and Barbara is shown to a parking space by the young helpers. Ben, pale and straight-faced but all eyes, is in the front of the mini

*next to her. The car parks, Ben and Barbara get out and
Barbara locks up. Ben looks around him, breathes in
deeply, coughs.*

BARBARA.   More like it, eh, Benjamin? See your dad's car?

*As Ben is looking round, Dave's Volvo turns in through
the gate and comes to park a few spaces away.*

BEN.   There! There they are.

BARBARA.   An' you don't have to be scared of a smile, you
know! You've got a Jamaica sky for it!

*Ad lib greetings and hugs from Lyn, Dave and Sally. Ben
is quiet and unresponsive.*

LYN.   *To Barbara.* Do him the world of good. Thanks
ever so much. Not so easy fixing, then?

They are walking towards the arena.

BARBARA.   It was not. An' I'm on my best behaviour!
Shows her shoulder bag. Half the pharmacy I've got in
here. But we got to be back by six or this girl's out of a
job!

*As they walk towards the arena and the sound of the
tannoy, Ben sees a father and son with two sheep dogs. He
puts his hands in his pockets and walks on into the arena –
looking small and frail, pale and vulnerable.*

BARBARA.   See – God made more'n one dog in this world,
Benjamin.

BEN.   Not for me, He never.

*They come to a vantage point where a sweep of country-
side can be seen beyond the field. They stop.*

DAVE.   They stopped 'em building over Eastchurch, then.

BEN.   *Still flatly.* Yeah? *He takes a deep breath, holds
himself ready to cough, but doesn't. His head raises a
fraction. He looks at the view again.* Good.

Dr. Skellman's cottage

Still Saturday morning, while Ben is at the trials. On the table there are books of chemical formulae, a few test tubes in a rack, and several notebooks. Lesley Skellman is writing in an exercise book. Charmaine is there, sitting at a home computer she has brought with her. Dr. Skellman throws down her pen, Charmaine looks up.

DR. SKELLMAN.   Come on! Come On! What aren't I seeing?

Dr. Skellman sighs, goes to the piano. She plays some energetic Mozart.

CHARMAINE.   Strewth, no time for that, Les. We got a kid to save! You've got an antidote to find!

DR. SKELLMAN.   It's supposed to help – bashing out your frustration.

She plays a phrase from a slow movement.

This is for thinking . . .

CHARMAINE.   No, keep thinking quick! *Comes over to the piano.* Go on, do the fast bit again.

Dr. Skellman frowns, but obliges.

CHARMAINE.   *Watches her fingers.* Got a theory!

Dr. Skellman stops.

CHARMAINE.   See it's all in here when you play. *Taps her forehead.* They know where they're going, your fingers. One note's joined onto the next, they're all series, sequences, aren't they? Archipelagos. You've learnt 'em.

DR. SKELLMAN.   Arpeggios. Of course I've learnt them.

Charmaine goes back to her computer keyboard.

CHARMAINE.   *At her computer.* It's different here. *She hunts for the keys to enter 'Compound D22' which we see on the display*. They don't even teach you to type first. Your finger looks for every single one.

Dr. Skellman folds her arms, stares at Charmaine, wants her to get to the point.

CHARMAINE.   What I've seen, that's what you're doing with the antidote. Formulas, series of 'em. Sequences. Learnt. Known links, like your fingers going fast. This leads to this, leads to this, same key, no question, tra-la-la. *She hums the fast Mozart, dances her fingers.* Mathematical. Now, put the first element of the D22 formula in here. *She copies a formula from a notebook onto the screen.* And then hunt round for the next link, don't think it's anywhere already . . . Forget strings . . .

Dr. Skellman stares at her.

CHARMAINE.   Might find the right tune, then. *Scratches her head.*

East Kent Trials

We are very aware of the silence, and of the two-note whistling and the commands of a boy working his dog. The large and attentive crowd is watching the difficult manoeuvre where one of a pair of marked sheep is being separated from the other seven in the shedding ring. Ben, Lyn, Dave and Barbara are sitting on a hillock watching with the rest.

BARBARA.   *Whispers to Ben.* What's he doing, that one?

Ben doesn't reply: He's staring at the boy working with the dog, and yet he's miles away.

DAVE.   Shedding. Got to get one o' them red-collared sheep shed from the rest.

BARBARA.   That what Ben does?

DAVE.   Ben and . . . *Nods.* Ben and a dog.

Barbara looks at Ben: still he stares. We watch the manoeuvre to a successful conclusion.

DAVE.   *In close up – to Barbara*. Done well. Give him ten. Just a good pen now and he'll have it. *He turns to Ben. But Ben isn't there.*

DAVE.   Ben? Where's that boy?

Dr. Skellman's cottage

Lesley Skellman, deep in her calculations, looks up and dictates to Charmaine at the computer keyboard.

DR. SKELLMAN.   O.K . . . It doesn't follow, but try taking out the phosphorous element – at this stage.

Charmaine does so, searching for keys. They look at the screen – which we don't see.

CHARMAINE.   Come on! Come on!

DR. SKELLMAN.   Now. Right. Store that.

She goes back to her notebooks with an air of hope.

A tourist spot in London, where Bill and Iraj met previously

Tourists and cameras abound. Iraj is making a pretence at tourist interest in a statue or a plaque. Adam comes up to him.

ADAM.   I hate these places.

IRAJ.   *Looking round nervously*. What about me?

ADAM.   *Shrugs*. This is your show. You got it?

IRAJ.   At great cost. *Takes a thermos flask from an airline bag*. Take care, it's lethal.

ADAM.   *Taking the flask*. So they reckon.

IRAJ.   This will really help. Match it with something going out from Britain and you've got a huge story.

A photographer approaches, of Middle-Eastern appearance.

ADAM.   That'll be the day!

The photographer takes a picture, indicates that he'd like one of them together. He takes another picture quickly.

IRAJ.   *Hand up at his face.* No, thank you. *He disappears in the crowd.*

Adam stares at the photographer.

ADAM.   You got a card? *He moves towards him.*

The photographer runs away.

East Kent Trials

TANNOY.   *(oov.)* Er, if anyone sees young Ben Westcott – Dave Westcott's boy – we'd like him brought here to the Public Address Box please. Thank you.

Lyn comes out of the P.A. Box and finds Dave. They've drawn a blank: stare at one another, Sally, Barbara.

LYN.   Police!

DAVE.   Hang on a minute . . .

LYN.   Hang on? Police!

J.M. Chemicals – Dr. Skellman's laboratory

What we see now is through a microscope. A yellow substance with a distinctive pattern of organisms is on a slide when a droplet of a clear liquid is introduced. The yellow blob is attacked, begins turning itself to a clear substance with changed patterns. We pull back to see Dr. Skellman at her microscope, watched by Charmaine.

DR. SKELLMAN.   So far, so good.

CHARMAINE.   We gonna be in time for that kid?

Dr. Skellman shrugs.

CHARMAINE.   A bit of hope, though? A little titchy bit?

DR. SKELLMAN.   *Finally permitting herself.* A bit. A little titchy bit ...

CHARMAINE.   We can tell Superman he helped.

Dr. Skellman frowns.

CHARMAINE.   Showing us where the can was. Convincing you! He's coming with his little sample.

DR. SKELLMAN.   A bit of him goes a very long way.

CHARMAINE.   Like his little sample!

East Kent Trials

The car parking field. A large police car is there with a driver and a tough W.P.C. *Dave, Lyn, Sally and Barbara are being questioned.*

W.P.C.   *To Barbara.* There's no way anyone else would have taken him back? There's not a minibus or anything?

BARBARA.   No, just him and me. And he's got to be back at six for his injection.

W.P.C.   *Looks at her watch.* There's been no-one hanging around? No one suspicious?

DAVE.   No. We know 'em all here.

W.P.C.   That's not the same thing at all.

LYN.   One minute he was there, the next minute he was gone.

BARBARA.   See, he's ... very ill ...

W.P.C.   *Reaches into the car for the radio.* O.K. I'll need a full description. He can't have got far.

The river near Egypt Creek

Alice is on the foreshore at low tide. She is throwing timbers useful for burning up above the high water line. Jem is with her. She throws a piece of planking up and takes a long look at a figure silhouetted on the sea wall.

ALICE.   Mister? Here, Ben – that's never you, is it?

BEN.   *Runs down to her.* Nan!

ALICE.   *Hugs him.* Ben! My dear old Ben. Where's your dad, or your mum?

BEN.   *Shaking his head.* Not here. I'm on my own.

ALICE.   You out of that hospital? They let you out, mister?

BEN.   No. I've come out, took myself out and I'm not going back. Not never ...

ALICE.   Here, hold your horses! What are you up to? You've not ...?

BEN.   I've come here, Nan. I've come back here. I'm not finishing up anywhere 'cept on the marshes ...

Alice's house – the room

Ben is sitting in a chair, Alice dosing him with a mixture.

ALICE.   Finishing up? What a cartload of clap-trap! Not while I'm around, you're not finishing up. Now, right down with it!

Ben swallows the mixture.

ALICE.   But it's not up to me, mister. It's up to your father. Your father's got to make the decision; not me – and not you.

BEN.   It's my life i'n it? I'm deciding. No-one's gonna make me go back there! No-one, Nan. Not even you.

ALICE.   *Shakes her head*. I shall have to put it to your father, Ben – and what's your mother going to say? You know what she reckons to me!

BEN.   Don't care. Don't care what you say. I've come out, and I'm staying out.

ALICE.   *Shakes her head*. Your father, mister. He's the one to . . .

BEN.   Nan! I'm not messing about. *The pain takes him again*. I'm not dying in that hospital!

Jem barks outside. Alice looks out of the window. We see a police car arriving.

BEN.   *Jumping up*. All right, you ask my dad. But don't tell them! Nan, I'll never forgive you if you tell them. *Looks round desperately*. Nan .. !

Alice looks.

ALICE.   Oh, strike me down for a stupid, wicked old woman. What have I come to here?

The police car hoots.

Outside Alice's house

The w.p.c. comes to the door, Jem barking round it. Alice comes to the door.

ALICE.   Lie down, Jem! Lie down.

Jem stops and stands as the w.p.c. walks over to Alice.

w.p.c.   Mrs. Westcott? Alice Westcott?

ALICE.   Why? *She looks beyond the w.p.c. in a good display of inquisitive innocence.*

W.P.C.   Sorry to trouble you. Have you seen your grandson? *Her walkie-talkie squawks unintelligibly: she switches it off.* Benjamin Dave Westcott. You seen him this afternoon at all?

ALICE.   My grandson? Ben? No! Why should he ..?

The W.P.C. *practically pushes past her to come in.*

I'm very busy ...

Alice's house – the room

W.P.C.   Aren't we all? *The* W.P.C. *looks round – sees the cup. As if drinking tea was suspicious.* Ah! Interrupt your cuppa?

ALICE.   Could you say what's going on? Ben's in hospital, up in London. He's ...

W.P.C.   Was. He was. But he's gone missing. Sorry to be John Blunt. Very close to you, they said.

ALICE.   Gone missing ..?

W.P.C.   *Surveying all the bags and bottles.* What's all this? Herbs, is it? Private cures?

ALICE.   Nature's way. Not against any law.

The W.P.C. *looks doubtful.*

W.P.C.   *Takes a last look around.* Well, you see a sign of him, you get in touch, Mrs. Westcott.

Alice nods. The W.P.C. *goes.*

ALICE.   Bye-bye. *She shuts the door.*

W.P.C. *leaves – crosses the bridge. We hear the police car drive away, to the barking of Jem. Alice watches it through the window, then she pulls out the truckle bed, which has Ben on it.*

ALICE.   You all right, mister? There's a hard one, eh?

BEN.   Yeah. Dragon! You did well, Nan.

ALICE.   Mister! Only till your father comes.

J.M. Chemicals – main entrance

The car park is empty as is customary on Saturday morning, with the exception of Charmaine's car parked near the main doors. The security guard is shutting the gates behind Adam, who has just arrived in his Fiat. Stephen West approaches the main entrance in his car, in time to see Adam getting out of his and being greeted by Charmaine at the door, who takes him inside. West pulls out of his swerve-in towards the gates and drives on past.

King Henry's Hospital – Walt Disney Ward – Sister's office

Mr. Murray-Mott and Sister O'Hara are carpeting Barbara James.

SISTER O'HARA.   Adam What's-his-name! That's it, Nurse, isn't it? You feed the stuff to your boyfriend, and he makes up a fine old story. Then you take the boy down to the country for episode two: 'Country Boy Back Home : Re-Union Before he Dies'. I can see tomorrow's heart-breaking pictures from here.

BARBARA.   No. It wasn't . . . .

SISTER O'HARA.   Oh, didn't we do the persuading to take him? Good for his spirits, good for his soul. Well, it's doing nothing for his body, my girl, is it?

MR. MURRAY-MOTT.   We had hopes of a breakthrough in this case. And now you've lost our patient! I'm sorry, Nurse, I shall have to recommend that you're suspended.

Barbara stares at Sister O'Hara, then makes up her mind about something and goes.

King Henry's Hospital – nurses' locker room

Barbara comes into the small locker room, and with a key from her key ring she opens her locker. She takes out a cardigan, a pair of flat work shoes – and her photo album, which arrests her. She weighs the photo album in her hand, almost absently pushes the locker shut as she hurries out of the room.

King Henry's Hospital – Walt Disney Ward

The usual crowded hustle and bustle. Barbara comes in and goes over to Ben's bed. She looks in his locker and finds his photo album. She opens it, and we see her look at a picture of Duke, and then at the picture of Ben with Alice. She stares at it.

LEE.   What you got there? You nickin' the evidence? 'E's done a runner, ol' Ee-aye!

BARBARA.   *Shakes her head before putting the album back.* Just lookin' at it.

Alice's house

Still Saturday afternoon, and the sun shining. Ben, beginning to look better already, is playing with Jem in front of the house. Alice is watching from the doorway, riven with doubts about Ben being there.

BEN.   Walk! Lie-down! Walk! Lie-down! Jem, lie-down! He's getting it, Nan.

ALICE.   *A distant interest – she's too worried about him being there.* Gentle! Keep the edge out of your voice.

BEN.   *Gentler.* Walk. Lie-down.

ALICE.   He'll obey right enough. *To herself.* Hard part's knowing which orders to give!

Ben throws a ball he has been holding out to Jem's left.

BEN.   Fetch it!

As Jem runs Ben whistles his 'go left' note.

BEN.   Great! He'll get it. He'll associate it, see? Good boy, good Jem! You'll get it, won't you, boy?

ALICE.   When you're out of hospital, he'll learn.

BEN.   *Stands up, to Alice.* I'm out now. I'm better already. Your stuff's magic, Nan.

ALICE.   Yeah, an' they'll have me for a witch! And think of your dad, Ben. And your mum. They'll be going through nightmares. I should never have ...

BEN.   Nan, you've got to!

ALICE.   Ben, it's all wrong, this.

BEN.   Do a deal! Do a deal, eh? One night. Rest of today and one night out here. One night, a bit in the fields with Jem in the morning ...

We hear the distant toot of Dave's car.

BEN.   *Gets past Alice, into the house.* That's someone! Come on! One night. You reckon your cures, don't you? *He disappears inside.*

Alice, in a terrible quandary, watches as Dave's Volvo drives up.

Inside Alice's house

There is no sign of Ben. Dave is at the table. He puts his head in his hands.

DAVE.   It was like someone waved a magic wand. One second he was watching, the next he was gone: vanished into thin air.

Above Dave's head, Alice is looking round. There is a gap between the truckle and Alice's bed. On the table at which

Dave is sitting are the makings of Ben's herbal potion, and a cup.

DAVE.   As if it was planned, like. Our Ben! And Lyn reckons he's been snatched.

ALICE.   No!

DAVE.   *Distressed at the thought.* If he has ..! He never made a sound.

ALICE.   He's all right, Davey.

DAVE.   Yeah, they're all saying that. All smiles and grip your arm. "We'll find him." Then you wait and they don't! *He can't finish.*

ALICE.   I said, he's all right, son.

DAVE.   *Looks at her.* What you saying?

ALICE.   I'm saying, trust my instinct, an old woman's instinct . . .

DAVE.   Mum, you know something I don't?

ALICE.   Only what I know. He's all right Davey. I can feel it . . .

Dave sees the herbal makings on the table. He looks at them, looks at Alice, frowns, look round the room, over to the truckle. We hear the sound of a helicopter, low. It is close and low enough to distract. Both Dave and Alice run to the door.

Outside Alice's house

A police helicopter sweeps across their part of the marsh, then off out and along the line of the river.

DAVE.   It's like the blessed news!

Alice looks at him. He holds her stare for a couple of beats.

ALICE.   Get off home to Lyn.

Dave goes to his car. Puzzled, he gets in and drives off, staring at her in his rear-view mirror.

Road by the Old Customs Houses, afternoon

Stephen West's car drives up with Brit in the front passenger seat. They get out, go over to the old houses.

Old Customs Houses – upstairs room,

We hear the sound of nails being ripped out of the door. Brit and West come in.

BRIT.   *Looking at the cache.* Still all right. An' plenty of room for what else you got.

WEST.   Might not even have to come in. Depends on the timing. Right. Now. Those women . . .

BRIT.   *Shakes his head.* Not here. How long, two weeks? No –

WEST.   Not two weeks. Indefinite. The one with the hair, she's in with the Press and linking him with this stuff. There'll be a searchlight on all this round here by the time she's done.

BRIT.   So, what you saying?

WEST.   For keeps. And two birds with one stone if you can.

BRIT.   I like them old sayings.

Barbara's flat, Sunday

Barbara carries a mug of coffee through from the kitchen into the living room. She has an ordnance survey map under her arm. She sits to drink her coffee, opening the map.

BARBARA.   Fleetham. *Finds it*. And Westcotts' Farm.

Her finger nail starts tracing a route on the map.

Martouf's Mercedes – A2

The car is driving along the A2, a chauffeur at the wheel. In the back, Martouf is on the car phone.

MARTOUF.   It's a ship called 'Colonial Star' – you should remember a name like that, Sir Richard – leaving the Pool of London tonight at 23.45. You rendezvous with her, off Fleetham, at half-past midnight. Customs cleared and can't be stopped, so there'll be no talk of coastguards, eh? Get alongside while she's under way and transfer your full cargo of canisters.

Martouf listens to Sir Richard, idly looking at glossy photographs of Iraj and Adam, taken at the tourist spot.

MARTOUF.   Excellent. Think of the look on your bank manager's face. As for other problems, one has been dealt with, the second – as good as. And I rely on you not to make yourself a third.

Dr. Skellman's laboratory

DR. SKELLMAN.   Charmaine!

Charmaine comes in carrying 'The News'.

DR. SKELLMAN.   Don't jump, don't shout, don't dance, don't sing. Don't move a muscle in celebration . . .

CHARMAINE.   You've found a pair of tights without holes.

DR. SKELLMAN.   Nearly as good. It's there. The antidote. I'm . . . reasonably, fairly, very confident . . .

CHARMAINE.   Lesley! *Without enthusiasm*. That's great!

DR. SKELLMAN.   It is for that boy. If it works. And it will. I'll stick my scientist's neck out and say it's going to work!

CHARMAINE.   Except there isn't a boy. Not at King
   Henry's. He's gone, disappeared. Shazam! Don't you
   ever read a newspaper?

DR. SKELLMAN.   *Takes the paper.* So where is he?

The lane to Egypt Creek

*Open with a close-up of Ben's glowing face; pull back to
show him walking contentedly along the lane with Jem
scampering around him. Ben is refreshed and happy, living
for the moment. This is a trailing shot, with music, in
contrast to the city stress which ended Episode Four. Jem
barks at something in the hedgerow.*

BEN.   No! Stand, Jem. No!

Jem goes on barking, gets nearer to the hedge.

BEN.   Lie down, Jem! Lie down!

*But Jem barks on and dives into the hedge, sending a
family of wild geese scattering.*

BEN.   Jem! Bad boy!

*As he holds Jem he looks out at the river, remembering
Duke.* You still got a way to go. But, come on . . .

Contentedly again, Ben walks on to Alice's house.

Alice's house

*Ben is sitting up at the table drinking his herbal medicine.
Alice is watching him closely.*

ALICE.   You're a different boy, mister, you know that?
   What about pains? Any pains?

BEN.   Nope!

ALICE.   Honest to God?

BEN.   Honest to Nan!

He gets up, looks round, is being noble. Still . . .

ALICE.   *A couple of beats.* No. You sit down. Help me, but you're staying on, if you want to. I said it at the first: they don't have all the blessed answers. Not always, not for everything. But the minute you get a pain . . . You hear me?

Westcotts' farm

Tony cycles up on his bike.

TONY.   Wotcha!

SALLY.   Oh, wotcha.

TONY.   I . . . er . . . I'm . . . Sal . . .?

SALLY.   I know. You're sorry about Ben.

TONY.   Yeah. No news?

SALLY.   No.

Sally walks down the track, Tony next to her, keeping up.

TONY.   Don't want to hold you up, getting back.

SALLY.   Don't then.

TONY.   Just wanted to say I'm sorry about . . .

SALLY.   *Stops.* About Duke?

TONY.   Yeah, about Duke.

SALLY.   And that does it? Makes it all right?

TONY.   Eh?

SALLY.   I could've got him. You had to be the big man. Oh, I don't know.

TONY.   I don't get you.

Sally walks off. Tony cycles off towards the escarpment.

Road near escarpment

Barbara's Mini comes to the top of the escarpment.

BARBARA.   *Out of her window to Tony.* Excuse me. That Westcotts' farm down there?

TONY.   Yeah. That big place.

BARBARA.   What about Egypt Creek? That's got to be . . . over there, yeah?

TONY.   *At the car window.* Yeah. I'll show you. Turn your map round.

The White Swan

Brit's and Scot's Land Rover is parked a few vehicle lengths short of the pub. Adam's Fiat drives past it and parks outside, sounding the horn. Charmaine runs out to Adam's car, gets in.

Adam's car

CHARMAINE.   Wotcha, Superman!

ADAM.   You got a result?

CHARMAINE.   How are you, Charmaine? Great, thanks.

ADAM.   Is it . .?

CHARMAINE.   Yup. Same stuff. Killer-diller. You going to tell me where it came from, yours?

ADAM.   Later. Read all about it.

The Land Rover suddenly cuts in on the parked car. Doors slam and Brit and Scot jump out.

CHARMAINE.   *Bangs the dashboard.* You owe on this?

ADAM.   No.

Brit and Scot start running towards them, one on either side.

CHARMAINE.   Go on, then! These aren't after your autograph!

Adam throws the car into reverse, Charmaine leans across and locks Adam's door. Scot runs after them. Brit runs back to the Land Rover.

Fleetham Street and country lanes

A serious and dangerous car chase begins, the Fiat pursued by the Land Rover, which looks very likely to catch up, or run them off the road. The chase runs past J.M. Chemicals *and a small industrial area. We see a branch line electric train in one of the shots.*

Brit's and Scot's Land Rover

The chase is still in the industrial area. Brit is driving, the light of victory in his eyes.

SCOT.   Easy! Don't get pulled. We got 'em, the other side o' this!

Adam's car

Adam is frustrated at lack of engine power, Charmaine, frightened, yet thrilled by the chase. The Land Rover comes very close.

ADAM.   Come on! Come on!

END OF EPISODE FIVE

EPISODE SIX

Industrial area – road past J.M. Chemicals

Adam's Fiat races through, with Brit's and Scot's Land Rover in close pursuit. Repeat the closing sequence from the end of Episode Five.

Interior of Adam's car

Seen from Charmaine's point of view in the front of Adam's car, they round a bend to come up against a closed level crossing.

ADAM.   No!

Interior of Brit's and Scot's Land Rover

BRIT.   Gotcha!

Interior of Adam's car

Still from Charmaine's point of view, we see the blocked road. To the side of the level crossing there is a small track and a five-foot-high tunnel looking like a water culvert, impossibly low.

CHARMAINE.   Down there! Quick!

ADAM.   Can't!

CHARMAINE.   Yes you can!

She grabs the wheel and forces the car left.

Go on!

ADAM.   You trying to kill us?

Adam ducks his head as they go for a certain smash.

The level crossing

Adam's Fiat shoots under the tunnel with nothing to spare. Running down into it, it looks to the eye as if nothing could get under – but saloon cars can. The Land Rover tries to follow.

Interior of Brit's and Scot's Land Rover

No dialogue. They are stuck under bridge.

Interior of Adam's car

CHARMAINE.   I go under there a lot.

ADAM.   *Looks at Charmaine's hair.* Yeah!

Country lane

Adam's Fiat drives off unpursued down an empty lane.

A crossroad

This is a small crossroad, of lanes rather than roads. Barbara's car is stopped there. Adam drives past and reverses back.

ADAM.   What you doing here, then?

Looks into Barbara's car, sees her map.

BARBARA.   None of your business!

She crashes her own gears and drives off. Adam watches her go.

ADAM.   She knows something. She's after that kid.

CHARMAINE.   Yeah, and someone's after us!

ADAM.   Where's a phone? Got a feeling about this.
A journalist's nose.

Charmaine looks at his nose critically.

The top of the escarpment – by a phone booth

*Adam's Fiat is parked tight to the available bushes,
keeping out of sight. Charmaine is in it. Adam comes from
the phone booth over to the car, looking shocked.*

CHARMAINE.   What's he say?

ADAM.   The Embassy guy who gave me the chemical.
They've found him ...

CHARMAINE.   Not nice?

ADAM.   Not nice at all.

CHARMAINE.   *Looks all round.* And us!

ADAM.   Get lost. Lie low for a few days, Bill reckons.
Where's your friend?

CHARMAINE.   King Henry's, working on the antidote.

ADAM.   Leave a message on her machine. It's all going
off. And it's the same stuff. It's all tied in. If we can
find that kid ...

CHARMAINE.   Police?

ADAM.   *Shakes his head.* Front page!

CHARMAINE.   My name in the paper! Long as it's not
under 'Deaths'!

J.M. Chemicals–Johnson–Marshall's office

JOHNSON-MARSHALL.   Got away! Couple of cowboys!
Couldn't catch my mother round the sofa. Well, keep
looking. Where's Skellman?

WEST.   *Shrugs.* Not in today. Not at home, either.

JOHNSON-MARSHALL.   She's a soft option. It's that reporter.

WEST.   They're all out for him. He won't publish.

JOHNSON-MARSHALL.   You all set for tonight?

WEST.   *Nods.* Just doing the final check on the boat. Everything else is lined up.

JOHNSON-MARSHALL.   So it's just today. Then we're in the clear.

King Henry's Hospital – research lab

Dr. Skellman is at a bench with a female technician and some sophisticated apparatus: with tubes and retorts, a small electric motor and computerised display screens. A stream of clear bubbling liquid is passing continuously through the apparatus. Dr. Skellman inserts an electric needle into a piece of tissue in a kidney dish.

DR. SKELLMAN.   O.K.

The technician switches on the current. Their eyes go to the screen.

DR. SKELLMAN.   That's it.

The fishing yacht

The yacht is moored at Gillingham Pier. Ted is at his small galley, frying a meal. Brit comes on board. Sniffs.

BRIT.   *Helps himself to a piece of fried bread from the edge of the stove.* Army marches on its guts! Bit soggy.

TED.   Fell in the bilge.

BRIT.   Ya!

Brit spits it out: gulps a mouthful of Ted's tea.

BRIT.   Right, listening? It's tonight. Rendezvous in the river, with the 'Colonial Star' off Fleetham, half-past twelve. You come alongside, transfer the stuff, then back here.

TED.   That's tricky with a river running.

BRIT.   *Gives him an envelope.* That's for tricks.

Brit dips a piece of bread in Ted's fried egg.

TED.   *Opens the envelope, thumbs the money, shakes his head.* You know I'm putting my ticket on the line for this. Get stopped, we could all go down for six months ...

BRIT.   You're joking! Get stopped, be six years, minimum.

Another junction of country lanes

We are getting further from Fleetham, more remote. Barbara's Mini pulls up. We see her consulting her map before driving off.

A dyke near Egypt Creek, same afternoon

Ben is lying by the dyke, his hand in the water, tickling for a stickleback. He is more tanned. Further along the dyke, Alice is gathering a cress-like plant from the water, while Jem forages on his own. Ben comes up with a stickleback in the hollow of his hand.

BEN.   Got you. *He looks at the fish closely.* Hey, ten-spined! *He puts his hand back just below the water surface and the fish darts off.* See that, Nan? Ten-spined stickleback.

ALICE.   I'm doin' well an' all, mister. Fetch my bag will you?

Ben gets up. Calls to Jem.

BEN.   Come by, Jem. Come by!

Jem runs to him.

BEN.   How about that, then?

ALICE.   It's your day, all right. Bag's up by the meadowsweet.

BEN.   Come on, boy. By me.

Ben jumps the dyke and goes out of sight behind some tall reeds, Jem going with him. Alice watches him go. She shakes her head at what she's doing and her lips move. Coming back to her plants, she bends to finger a leaf from a spotted orchid: inspects it closely.

BARBARA.   That the orchid family?

Alice spins round. Barbara has approached unseen and unheard from the other side of the sea wall. Alice throws a quick look to see whether Ben is out of sight.

ALICE.   *Staring at Barbara in partial recognition.* Sorry . . . You creep up quiet on a person.

BARBARA.   *Laughs.* Sensible shoes. I'm the nurse from King Henry's.

ALICE.   *Now she remembers.* Oh . . .

BARBARA.   I saw you visiting. Nice to meet you. *Her eyes start looking all round.*

Alice squints. What else has the nurse seen? Ben, coming back, spots Barbara through the reeds and flowers. He drops down flat with the bag. Jem comes and lies down flat next to him. They're like two dogs guarding the sheep.

BEN.   *Whispers.* Yeah! Good boy, Jem. Lie still.

ALICE.   It's good of you to come so far, all on your day off.

Alice tries to turn Barbara towards the house.

BARBARA.   It's not my day off – they suspended me.

ALICE.   No . . .

BARBARA.   *Looking at the spotted orchid plant, fingering the leaf.* Same sort of roots, him and me. And he's around here somewhere. *Eyeing Alice.* Stands to sense – he's got to be, hasn't he?

ALICE.   Oh, if only he was.

BARBARA.   *Indicates the plants Alice has.* What's this? Those cures you're collecting? Herbs, and everything?

ALICE.   Oh, little things for the snuffles, just nice smells . . .

BARBARA.   *Frowning at the water plants, which are a long way from attractive pot pourri.* And the rue? You collect the rue, Mrs. Westcott?

ALICE.   What for?

BARBARA.   Old remedy for poisoning . . .

ALICE.   Lord no, girl! Nothing serious like that . . .

BARBARA.   They're serious up at King Henry's. Word says. Some sort of breakthrough.

Alice stares at her.

BARBARA.   Here! *She unpins her nurse's badge from her shoulder-bag flap.* Royal College of Nursing. You see him, you give him this. From Barbara. Tell him to come and give it back to me, because it's no good to me till he does . . .

Alice stares at her, shakes her head, but takes the badge on Barbara's insistence. Jem barks, comes bounding out.

BARBARA.   Jem! That's Jem, eh? I reckon.

ALICE.   Yes, I reckon it is. Jem! Jem! Here boy. Been off after something. Jem!

Jem hesitates. Will he go back to Ben and reveal him, or to Alice? Ben, still hidden, shoos him silently.

ALICE.   Jem! Here, I say, boy! Here, boy!

Jem runs to her.

BARBARA.   There's a lovely boy. *Goes to pet him.* Where you been, boy, what's over there?

ALICE.   *Laughs.* Oh, rabbits! Come on, let's get you a cup of tea, set you on your way . . .

Alice leads Barbara off towards her house. Jem follows. Ben watches them go, with much to think about. He rolls over on his back and shuts his eyes against the sun, frowning.

Alice's house – the room

Alice and Ben are up at the table eating rabbit stew for supper. Nothing is said at first. When Alice addresses her plate, Ben looks across at her. When Ben addresses his, Alice looks across at him. Finally, their worrying eyes meet, by accident. Alice feels in her pocket and brings out Barbara's badge, puts it on the table between them.

BEN.   Reckon she's coming back?

ALICE.   Dunno, mister.

They eat on.

ALICE.   Dunno about a lot of things.

Outside Alice's house

After tea. Ben is sawing wood with Alice, using a twin saw. They get through a log and it falls to the floor.

ALICE.   Makes it easy. Just made for two, this is, mister.

Ben picks up another log, puts it in the trestle.

BEN. *Puffed.* Makes it easy?

ALICE. Here, you take good care. *She stops the saw.* How you feeling? Medicine soon.

BEN. *Starts the saw.* I'm all right. In here. *Points to his stomach.*

ALICE. *She starts the saw, then stops again.* Yeah, and I'm in a flummox, mister. Only done this for the best . . .

Ben tries to start the saw again but she won't have it.

ALICE. Biggest hitch of all in life, not being certain! Mind, I'm not going back on my word, no fear of that. No, it's your call. I'll go along with it whatever. But . . .

Carefully getting in time again they recommence sawing, but avoiding each other's eyes as soon as they're under way.

The sea wall and the Thames near Egypt Creek

Ben, in a thoughtful mood, head down like a scavenger on the foreshore, walks along with Jem. He stops, looks at the mud, catches Jem's collar when the dog makes for the water.

BEN. No, not there. Keep clear, boy.

We hear the engine of a police launch. Ben looks up. We see it coming along near to the shore. Still clutching Jem's collar, Ben pulls the dog down behind the decaying remains of a rowing boat, and watches the launch go by. A policeman with binoculars is surveying the shoreline. As the launch rounds a bend and goes out of sight, Ben, in a crouch, runs up over the sea wall into a field.

BEN. Come on, Jem, stay by! Stay by!

A field near Egypt Creek

Ben runs over the sea wall and into the field. There are sheep grazing, and Jem wants to chase them.

BEN.   No, lie still! Hear me!

Jem lies still.

Good boy.

Ben, picking up his thoughtful mood from before the launch came, lies on his back and stares up at the sky. Jem starts barking.

BEN.   Lie still, now.

Squinting in the sun, Ben sees what Jem persists in barking at. It is the approaching figure of Barbara.

BARBARA.   'Lo, Benjamin. Well! I knew you were around ...

BEN.   Yeah?

BARBARA.   I reckoned. So what are you doing here? Going to lie here hidden the rest of your life?

BEN.   Could do worse. Wasn't much of it left before.

BARBARA.   Oh, you're cured! Is that it? Well, that's good.

BEN.   Miles better than I was.

BARBARA.   Feeling miles better. Your nan's got some good stuff, oh yes. But curing's different, Benjamin. They've got a breakthrough now, you know that? Testing it all for you.

BEN.   *Defiant rather than rude.* And I'm not there.

BARBARA.   No, you're not there. But then it'd take a lot of guts to go back, wouldn't it? For the country boy.

Ben rolls onto his front, chews grass.

BARBARA.   Don't do it for me, mind. I'm going home soon – and I don't care if I come back or not. Depends on my badge, Benjamin, but it's no big deal. You'd be doing it for yourself.

BEN.   You've found me now. You'll tell them anyhow.

BARBARA.   *Shakes her head.* I'm leaving it to you.

Lay-by on the A2

Evening. A large Transit van is parked. Brit's and Scot's Land Rover drives into the lay-by. West is in it with them. The three get out while Scot pretends to check the Land Rover's tyres, keeping watch for a police patrol. Brit fishes in the Transit's exhaust pipe for its keys.

WEST.   Open up the back.

Scot does so. We see rows of canisters filling the transit. They are identical to D22, twenty plus of them. West takes a can down, untapes the seal and opens the lid. Inside, the can is filled with a look-alike to D22.

BRIT.   What's that?

WEST.   You could have it for your tea.

BRIT.   You saying they won't know the difference?

WEST.   Time they find out, it won't matter, will it?

He reseals the canister as Brit starts unrolling a plastic sticker to go along the side of the van.

Road by the Old Customs Houses

Charmaine and Adam approach the row of old houses from along the track, keeping a low profile. They are on foot.

CHARMAINE.   Why here? He did a runner miles from here.

ADAM.   *At the houses.* Sort of place he might hole up in . . .

CHARMAINE.   *Realising what they might find.* I'm not looking in there.

ADAM.   Keep a look out, then, while I have a nose around.

They separate, Adam to the houses, Charmaine towards the road. Adam sees the padlocked door, looks in through the window. Using a handy drainpipe and the window ledges, he looks in through the upstairs window. Intercut a shot of the tarpaulin and the identifiable end of one canister. Cut to Charmaine, returning from the road.

ADAM.   The canisters!

CHARMAINE.   Look out! Somebody's coming!

We see Brit arriving at the Old Customs Houses in the Land Rover, dressed with binoculars for bird-watching. He gets out, is very prominent as he makes sure everything is ready, pinning Charmaine and Adam down where they are.

J. M. Chemicals – front gate

Later that evening. Recognising Stephen West in the front, the security guard unlocks and lets the Transit van through the gates. It is driven by Scot. Along its side the new sticker reads 'J. M. Chemicals – Medical Supplies'. The van goes round to the side of the building.

The loading bay

The Transit van is backing up to the warehouse doors, still driven by Scot, West directing it.

Inside the warehouse

West goes to the cage and taps in the code to unlock it. Scot and West start taking out the real D22 to the Transit van in two-man carriable crates.

Gillingham Pier

*Ted comes along the pier with fishing rods, etc. He jumps
onto his boat, starts the engine, casts off, engages gear and
heads out of the moorings. A large rubber dinghy is tied up
behind.*

The warehouse

*Under a couple of local spotlights, the dummy D22 goes
into the cage as the real stuff gets taken out to the Transit
in the plastic crates. A couple of spare crates are thrown
into the van.*

Alice's house

*Alice, looking smaller and older in her thin dressing-gown,
tucks Ben into his truckle bed under the window.*

ALICE.   Night, mister. You been a quiet one, today.

BEN.   Yeah? I am sometimes.

ALICE.   And thank goodness for that, eh?

BEN.   Night, Nan.

ALICE.   Sweet dreams.

Ben stares at her, smiles, and turns away as if to sleep.

The river

*Ted's boat makes its way up river, only Ted aboard,
trailing the rubber dinghy.*

The pool of London

The 'Colonial Star' is casting off.

Meopham House, night

Lesley Skellman's car drives up to the front door.

Meopham House – the hall

DR. SKELLMAN.   Sorry it's so late. I knew you'd want to
know, Sir Richard. My antidote. I've come straight
from King Henry's ...

JOHNSON-MARSHALL.   Oh, yes?

DR. SKELLMAN.   It's a success. We can save that boy, we
think, if we can find him in time.

Meopham House – the library

*Lady Johnson-Marshall has her feet up on the settee,
dozing and wearing a Walkman. Between the two high-
backed fireside chairs is a table with a telephone on it. One
of these chairs has its back to us.*

DR. SKELLMAN.   What was the police reaction when you
reported the missing canisters?

JOHNSON-MARSHALL.   Oh! Busy people, Lesley. Very busy
people.

DR. SKELLMAN.   But we must be seen to be acting quickly
on these thefts. You gave your word, Sir Richard.

*Now we see who is in the armchair. Mr. Martouf's head
comes round the wing. He gets up.*

MARTOUF.   Ah, the Englishman's word. We're back to
that again. Notoriously unreliable, my dear. Notoriously
unreliable.

Now Lesley Skellman realises that she is in danger.

Alice's house

*The room is in darkness, with Alice asleep on her bed. Not
snoring but breathing deeply with regular sighs. Ben's
truckle bed is under the window, through which a clouded
moon is shining. Ben is lying there awake. He coughs,*

*stares up at the moon. From his point of the view we see
the moon, and clouds crossing it. Ben stares hard and long
at one big cloud which covers the moon. Looking over at
Alice, Ben seems to make up his mind. He gets out of bed,
dresses silently, and, while Alice continues to sleep, tiptoes
across the room to the mantelpiece. The cloud passes across
the moon, and a bounced shaft of moonlight glints on
Barbara's badge. With a last look round at Alice, Ben
takes the badge, pockets it, and quietly goes out. (oov.)
Jem barks briefly. Alice stirs, shifts, stops her noisy
breathing. Jem stops barking, Alice shifts again. Are her
eyes open or not?*

The marshes

*In the clouded moonlight, Ben half-walks, half-runs
towards his home. But with the exertion he begins to cough
and a sudden pain comes: similar symptoms to his initial
illness.*

BEN.   No!

Road near the Old Customs Houses

*The Transit van is parked with the rear doors open. West,
Brit and Scot are loading the van with crates of canisters
from the house. Charmaine and Adam are watching.*

The river

The 'Colonial Star' is coming down river, lights blazing.

The marshes

*Ben staggers on with some difficulty. He comes to a halt
again. Coughs. Sighs deeply, is going to lie down, like
Duke did. But as he sits something hurts under him. He
pulls it out. It is Barbara's badge. He pulls himself up and
goes on.*

Road near the Old Customs Houses

Ben staggers along, nearly home, and comes across the canister-loading. He watches in the moonlight as a crate is carried to the van. Involuntarily, he coughs, and tries to stifle it.

SCOT. Wha's that?

West, Brit and Scot freeze. Ben stares, scared, with his hand over his mouth.

BRIT. It's nothing. Come on!

They carry on loading. Ben is skirting them carefully when he is grabbed by Adam, hand over his mouth.

CHARMAINE. 'S'all right! And you're Ben!

Ben takes Adam's hand from his mouth, slowly, indicating that he won't shout.

BEN. What's that stuff?

ADAM. Chemicals. Dangerous.

BEN. Smuggling it?

CHARMAINE. When they're not slinging it in the water.

Ben stares at it, realisation dawning.

BRIT. *Bangs the van.* Come on! Job an' knock!

West, Scot and Brit get into the van and start it.

BEN. They're getting away!

The van heads for the river.

ADAM. Where's that lead?

BEN. *Coughs.* River. The jetty.

ADAM. They must have a boat.

CHARMAINE. Brain of Britain!

BEN.   Get my dad! My house is down there. *To Adam.*
There's a short cut, across the marshes. Come on,
I know it!

ADAM.   Get the police!

Ben starts off across the marshes.

BEN.   Come on!

*Charmaine runs off towards Westcotts' farm, Ben and
Adam head off across the dykes.*

The marshes

*Ben is leading Adam across the rough and dyke-crossed
terrain.*

Westcotts' farmhouse, night

*Charmaine runs up to the darkened house and starts
banging on the door.*

The jetty

*Ted's boat is moored in the river. The Transit van arrives,
Brit, West and Scot jump out.*

Westcotts' farm

We see lights come on.

Westcott's farm – front door

*Before Lyn opens the door she puts the chain across, pulls
her dressing-gown close.*

CHARMAINE.   *(oov.)* Come on! Come on! Please!

Lyn opens the door, sees Charmaine.

LYN.   Who is it?

CHARMAINE.   You Ben's mum?

LYN.   Yes. Why? Don't say – ?

Opens door. Dave arrives, pulling on trousers.

DAVE.   What is it?

CHARMAINE.   Your boy! He's out there, by the old houses. There's a gang, with stolen chemicals.

LYN.   Ben!

CHARMAINE.   He's watching them.

DAVE.   Damn fool!

CHARMAINE.   We must phone the police!

LYN.   Of course. Come in!

Dave is pushing out as Charmaine squeezes in and Lyn turns to get to the phone.

DAVE.   And the hospital!

Lyn runs into the living room, Dave runs out.

Outside Westcotts' farmhouse

Dave runs out to his car with his flashlight.

Westcott's farmhouse – living room

Lyn is at the phone, Charmaine by her.

LYN.   *To Charmaine.* Sir Richard Who?

CHARMAINE.   *Takes the phone, speaks in to it.* Johnson-Marshall. Sir Richard Johnson-Marshall. Yeah, that's the one. Well, you get there an' all – but out here first! *To Lyn.* Right, now, hospital!

Another part of the marshes

Ben is still leading Adam across.

BEN.   Mind that! You're all right, they run parallel.

ADAM.   *Out of breath.* Good ... on you ...

BEN.   *Coughs.* Should know, shouldn't I?

The jetty

Ted's boat is moored off, unable to get closer due to the tide. A rubber dinghy with an outboard motor is being used to transfer one of the crates of canisters from the jetty to the boat. Brit is at the outboard. At the van, West and Scot are with crates.

Interior of Dave's car

On the road to the sea wall, trying too hard, Dave hits a pot-hole. There's a bang of a tyre going.

DAVE.   No! Blast!

The car is useless. Dave gets out and runs along the road.

The jetty

Ben and Adam arrive, stay concealed to see Brit arrive back at the jetty steps with the empty dinghy. A crate is ready on the jetty, with Scot and West back at the van. Brit ties up the dinghy, engine off, and runs up the steps. He can't carry the crate down alone.

BRIT.   Over here! Come on!

(oov.): Ship's hooter. Brit looks at his watch.

Come on!

He runs to the van to get help. Ben gets up out of cover.

ADAM.   Stay down!

Ben runs to the jetty steps, down them and starts untying the dinghy rope. But it's too tight. He starts to cough.

BEN.   Can't do it!

SCOT.   Wha's goin' on?

Adam breaks cover and runs down the jetty steps. Brit runs across from the van with Scot and West.

BRIT.   Come here, you!

Adam cuts the rope with a pocket knife, throws Ben into the dinghy and they push it off.

ADAM.   Quick! Push!

Ship's hooter, closer.

TED.   *From the boat.* Come on! We'll miss her!

BRIT.   *Down the jetty steps, reaching for the dinghy, getting hold of the rubber, but his hands slip.* Come back here, you!

Adam and Ben paddle out furiously with their hands.

WEST.   Bring that back!

BEN.   No! You killed my dog!

BRIT.   I'll kill you!

He starts stripping off his top combat jacket to dive into the water. Now we see the ship coming round the final bend.

SCOT.   Leave it! We're too late!

Ben is coughing in the dinghy. As we watch, the ship goes on past. The sound of a helicopter. We hear Ted start the engine of the fishing yacht.

BRIT.   You yellow – !

SCOT.   Beat it!

He runs off in one direction. Brit, after a final look round, runs off in another. We see West, turning to look inland in a panic. In the distance, at the top of the escarpment, we see a flashing blue light. A searchlight from a police launch lights up Ted's boat. West runs — into the arms of Dave.

DAVE.   Where's my kid? Eh?

Dave holds West in a strong and painful grip.

The police car has arrived, blue light still flashing. Scot is being pushed into it, next to Brit. West is being questioned by the van. Adam, Ben and Dave are at the head of the jetty steps.

ADAM.   He was great. You did well, Ben.

DAVE.   *Hugging Ben.* Now get well, eh?

Ben coughs.

DAVE.   I couldn't have made it in time. Where'd you get the strength for that run?

BEN.   Nan. And Barbara.

ADAM.   Barbara?

BEN.   She thought I didn't have the guts.

He takes Barbara's badge from his pocket, shows it on his palm.